THE ULTIMATE READ-ALOUD RESOURCE

LESTER L. LAMINACK

Making Every Moment Intentional and Instructional with Best Friend Books

■SCHOLASTIC

Credits

OWEN by Kevin Henkes. Copyright © 1993 by Kevin Henkes. Published by HarperCollins Children's Books, a division of HarperCollins Publishers.

JAMAICA'S FIND by Juanita Havill, illustrated by Anne Sibley O'Brien. Text copyright © 1986 by Juanita Havill. Illustrations copyright © 1986 by Anne Sibley O'Brien. Published by Houghton Mifflin Harcourt Publishing Company.

CROW CALL by Lois Lowry, illustrated by Bagram Ibatoulline. Text copyright © 2009 by Lois Lowry. Illustrations copyright © 2009 by Bagram Ibatoulline. Published by Scholastic Inc.

Excerpts and images from ALL THE PLACES TO LOVE by Patricia MacLachlan, illustrated by Michael Wimmer. Text copyright © 1994 by Patricia MacLachlan. Illustrations copyright © 1994 by Michael Wimmer. Reprinted by permission of HarperCollins Children's Books, a division of HarperCollins Publishers.

Excerpts and images from THE RECESS QUEEN by Alexis O'Neill, illustrated by Laura Huliska-Beith. Text copyright © 2002 by Alexis O'Neill. Illustrations copyright © 2002 by Laura Huliska-Beith. Reprinted by permission of Scholastic Inc.

Excerpts and images from DIARY OF A WORM by Doreen Cronin, illustrated by Harry Bliss. Text copyright © 2003 by Doreen Cronin. Illustrations copyright © 2003 by Harry Bliss. Reprinted by permission of HarperCollins Children's Books, a division of HarperCollins Publishers.

Excerpts and images from SNOW DAY! by Lester L. Laminack, illustrated by Adam Gustavson. Text copyright © 2007 by Lester L. Laminack. Illustrations copyright © 2007 by Adam Gustavson. Reprinted by permission of Peachtree Publishers.

THE BARN OWLS by Tony Johnston, illustrated by Deborah Kogan Ray. Illustrations copyright © 2000 by Deborah Kogan Ray. Published by Charlesbridge Publishing, Inc.

COME A TIDE by George Ella Lyon, illustrated by Stephen Gammell. Illustrations copyright © 1990 by Stephen Gammell. Published by Scholastic Inc.

IN NOVEMBER by Cynthia Rylant, illustrated by Jill Kastner. Illustrations copyright © 2000 by Jill Kastner. Published by Houghton Mifflin Harcourt Publishing Company.

THE OTHER SIDE by Jacqueline Woodson, illustrated by E. B. Lewis. Illustrations copyright © 2001 by E. B. Lewis. Published by G. P. Putnam's Sons, an imprint of Penguin Young Readers Group, a division of Penguin Random House.

PETER'S CHAIR by Ezra Jack Keats. Illustrations copyright © 1967 by Ezra Jack Keats. Published by Viking Children's Books, an imprint of Penguin Young Readers Group, a division of Penguin Random House.

ROSIE'S WALK by Pat Hutchins. Illustrations copyright © 1968 by Patricia Hutchins. Published by Aladdin, an imprint of Simon & Schuster Children's Publishing Division.

SATURDAYS AND TEACAKES by Lester L. Laminack, illustrated by Chris Soentpiet. Text copyright © 2004 by Lester L. Laminack. Illustrations copyright © 2004 by Chris Soentpiet. Published by Peachtree Publishers.

THREE HENS AND A PEACOCK by Lester L. Laminack, illustrated by Henry Cole. Illustrations copyright © 2011 by Henry Cole. Published by Peachtree Publishers.

TWILIGHT COMES TWICE by Ralph Fletcher, illustrated by Kate Kiesler. Illustrations copyright © 1997 by Kate Kiesler. Published by Houghton Mifflin Harcourt Publishing Company.

WILFRID GORDON MCDONALD PARTRIDGE by Mem Fox, illustrated by Julie Vivas. Illustrations copyright © 1984 by Julie Vivas. Published by Kane Miller Books.

HUNGRY HEN by Richard Waring, illustrated by Caroline Jayne Church. Illustrations copyright © 2001 by Caroline Jayne Church. Published by HarperCollins Children's Books, a division of HarperCollins Publishers.

ROLLER COASTER by Marla Frazee. Illustrations copyright © 2003 by Marla Frazee. Published by Houghton Mifflin Harcourt Publishing Company.

TANKA TANKA SKUNK! by Steve Webb. Illustrations copyright © 2004 by Steve Webb. Published by Scholastic Inc.

All rights reserved.

Publisher: Lois Bridges
Editor-in-Chief: Raymond Coutu
Development/production editor: Danny Miller
Video editor: Sarah Longhi
Cover designer: Eliza Cerdeiros
Cover/interior photographer: Bob Leverone
Interior designer: Maria Lilja

ISBN-13: 978-1-338-10925-2

2 3 4 5 6 7 8 9 10   40   25 24 23 22 21 20 19 18 17 16

For teachers and librarians
who understand
the importance and power
of reading aloud:

You ignite the passion.

For the authors and illustrators
of children's books:

You provide the fuel
that feeds the passion.

For young readers and writers:

You will change the world
through your passion.

Contents

Acknowledgments

Every book is the result of the efforts of many people. My name goes on the cover, but there are many people who worked tirelessly to make this happen. First, my Scholastic team: I am ever grateful to Lois Bridges, dear friend, staunch advocate, and insightful editor. Thank you for always seeing more in me than I see in myself. Ray Coutu, you have been a friend across many years and your insights with this project have been invaluable. You are a treasure. Sarah Longhi, I appreciate your diligence and careful attention to detail. Danny Miller, it has been a pleasure to craft my thoughts knowing they would be passing by your watchful eyes before making an appearance in the world. Brian LaRossa and Maria Lilja, what a pleasure it has been to brainstorm and banter as you work your magic with design.

And then …

I am always under the influence of the rhythm, the cadence, and the power of the voice of Mrs. Hand, the librarian who brought books to life for me. Reba Wadsworth, sister-friend, you have been a rock as I have found my footing through some tough times in life. You are always ready to listen and bounce ideas with me. #502Writers—Katie Stover, Karen Dawson Haag, Rebecca Shoniker—I am grateful for our semiannual gatherings where ideas take shape and words find their home on the page. I am grateful to the administration and faculty of the many schools I have had the pleasure of working with as these ideas have emerged. You have been instrumental in pushing me toward clarity. I am grateful to my dear friends at Shaner Elementary, Topeka, Kansas, for your trust, your questions, and your willingness to try something new. And I am especially grateful to Buffy Fowler and the team at Francine Delaney New School for Children in Asheville, North Carolina, for your unending willingness to partner with me when I have new ideas to explore.

And finally …

Steve, with you my light is brighter.

You know … more than coffee.

Welcome, Readers

Welcome, my fellow educators, to an exploration of the art and purpose of reading aloud. Please join me in an effort to make every experience with books intentional and instructional and like a relationship with a best friend. Join me in an effort to bring read-aloud back to a place of prominence in the lives of children. As you'll discover, the benefits are innumerable.

The interactive read-aloud is multifaceted. It lends itself to both extended chapter books as well as short text such as poetry, magazine articles, and short stories—and it accomplishes multiple, essential instructional goals simultaneously, including:

- Drawing *all* students into the text
- Capturing the interest of disengaged readers
- Expanding students' reading horizons by exposing them to new books, authors, and genres
- Furnishing background information
- Refining students' understanding of *text*—genre, format, literary elements, text structures, and features
- Promoting inquiry
- Promoting conversations using literary language
- Teaching essential strategic reading actions
- Encouraging students to view topics from multiple perspectives
- Improving listening comprehension
- Building academic vocabulary
- Deepening comprehension
- Modeling all aspects of thinking, talking, and writing about reading
- Developing insights into what writers do to support readers
- Demonstrating fluent reading
- Building an intellectual classroom community of readers
- Introducing and modeling collaborative conversations
- Addressing the requirements of higher standards
- Fostering a lifelong love of reading

Jim Flanagan is a fifth-grade teacher at a residential school in Philadelphia that serves primarily children of color from high-poverty neighborhoods. Jim knows well the benefits of the read-aloud because he begins every school morning with a 30-minute session. He explains what the read-aloud means to him and his students:

> A daily read-aloud in every classroom is the place to start reclaiming conversation. When we assemble together in our classroom as a school family, our family dinner is the read-aloud. Each morning, I greet all the kids as they walk in the room and gather around the big table by the windows. If it's bright enough outside, we keep the fluorescent lights off and just use the natural light and a few lamps to warm the pile of books in front of me and read.

> Most days the group discussion is insightful, poignant, humorous, and tender. You lay a foundation of interesting background knowledge and compelling stories, and the connections are made in a natural way. Exposing the students to so much, touching on so many topics, locations, and ideas, something always captures every child's interest. You pique their curiosity, and expose them to the broad range of what the world offers. There is ample opportunity for the kids to share during the read-aloud, just like there is in an authentic conversation. The teacher guides the conversation, and makes sure everyone is engaged and respectful, and that the kids participate and stay engaged. We share and learn about each other in ways we would otherwise never know—and that builds trust, which, in turn, builds love and respect.

Literature, language, and love—this is what a Best Friends interactive read-aloud offers, and you can't beat that!

When Books Become Best Friends

"That was the beginning of a lifelong journey in which books would shape and change me, making me who I was to become."

—CHARLES M. BLOW, *NEW YORK TIMES* OP-ED COLUMNIST

As I share read-alouds with both children and teachers, I take great pleasure in bringing a book to life through the use of voice, facial expressions, and body language. The merits of the experience and the sheer pleasure of bonding with children over a book seem obvious. In fact, reading aloud to children seems as natural as inhaling and exhaling.

Yet I have heard countless teachers express the need to justify time spent on read-aloud experiences in the instructional day. So in this book I hope to reveal the gift it can be in the lives of children and how the books that you read aloud can become Best Friend Books.

What Is a Best Friend Book?

Think about one of your best friends. Reflect on how you met and how your friendship developed. Even if you had an immediate connection, it is likely that your connection deepened over time—through shared experiences, common interests, earned trust, mutual respect, and a growing sense of knowing you can depend upon each other when things get difficult.

We have many friends and acquaintances, but our "best friends" are a treasure. We know and count on them in ways that transcend our other relationships.

A Best Friend Book (BFB) will be similar. You may feel an immediate connection to it—but it will take time and repeated visits for you to recognize the depth of what it has to offer. It is likely that your first visit will be connecting with the story line—the content. That must prove worthy of your attention; it must offer something of substance that will leave you thinking and wanting to revisit. More visits will likely result in small delights and discoveries along the way:

SPOTLIGHT ON
LESTER VIDEO
**Introduction to
Best Friend Books**
scholastic.com/BFBresources

THE TURN OF A PHRASE

This can best be described as an artful or unexpected way of saying something. For example, one might say, "That gives my nightmares nightmares" versus "That's creepy."

THE USE OF SPECIFIC CONCRETE NOUNS

Specific concrete nouns zero in to help the reader gain greater clarity. For example, the writer may say, "I sat on the porch in a metal chair." Now consider how the more specific concrete noun brings even greater clarity in this example: "I sat on the porch in a folding *aluminum rocker.*"

WELL-CHOSEN PRECISE VERBS

Precise or vivid verbs provide more specificity in the writing and give the reader a more precise image of what is happening. For example, the writer may say, "Sam *walked* three blocks to the store." Now, consider how the more precise, vivid verbs that follow evoke a better sense of how Sam feels on his trip to the store: "Sam [*waltzed* or *skipped* or *sprinted* or *trudged*] three blocks to the store."

THE DEVELOPMENT OF A CHARACTER

Writers develop and reveal characters in a number of ways. For example, the narrator can simply tell you: "Marcus was a large boy for his age, almost a head taller than any kid in kindergarten. His face was sprinkled with freckles, and he had a cowlick above his left eye that made his hair spike up despite his mother's fondness for hair gel." The writer may also develop the character slowly, revealing personality and attributes through the character's actions/reactions, thoughts, or dialogue. In addition, we may come to know a character by listening in on the dialogue of other characters.

THE ARTFUL USE OF DESCRIPTION

Description helps the reader create a sense of things, a sensory awareness. Artful description is well-placed detail that spotlights or assigns importance to an object, person, place, or action. For example, a writer may say, "Alice poured her morning coffee in her favorite cup and read the paper." But if that cup is of great importance and will have some significant role later in the story, you may find the writer drawing your attention toward the cup: "Alice took the cup from the cabinet and held it just a moment. The inside was stained from years of morning coffee. She ran her thumb over the chip on the rim where her grandfather had nicked it on the edge of the counter in his last days at home. Though she had seen it thousands of times, the image of Bugs Bunny always made her chuckle."

THE BALANCE OF DIALOGUE AND NARRATIVE

Think of the narrator in a story telling you everything from beginning to end. It can work. But the use of dialogue along with narrative gives the reader insight into the personality of the character. Dialogue can provide bits of the backstory or reveal plans for the future. A story told through dialogue only would read like a script for a play with no stage directions. Finding balance between the narrative and the dialogue of characters results in a more robust reading experience.

THE ARC OF THE STORY

Story moves through a series of events or scenes in a logical sequence. The most common way to think of a story arc is to move from the initiating event to rising action/tension, toward the climax, to falling action, and ending with a conclusion. You can explore this further in the diagram on page 69.

THE DEVELOPMENT OF AN ARGUMENT

Story can present opportunities to explore an argument. In these situations, we want to notice the character's stance on the topic. We want to be able to search back through the story and find examples in actions, reactions, thought, and dialogue to support the assertion. For example, let's assume two characters are playing in the park and they find a jacket near the swings. One character tries it on and decides to keep it, declaring "finders keepers." The other character insists they take the jacket to lost and found because some kid is going to get in trouble for losing that jacket.

WELL-PLACED SPECIFIC TEXT STRUCTURES TO ENGAGE THE READER AND EXECUTE THE AUTHOR'S INTENT

Think about five basic text structures (description, sequence, problem/ solution, cause/effect, compare/contrast) and how they can be used to move a story forward. For example, let's say a character is trying to make a decision about which of two items to purchase. In this situation, the writer may choose to have the character think through a compare/contrast scenario where the character thinks, "I could wear either pair to school, but if I choose these I could also wear them to the party on Friday…." Another option would be to consider a cause/effect scenario where the character thinks, "If I buy this one, all my money will be gone and then I couldn't go to…." You can find a printable graphic organizer for the Five Basic Text Structures That Help Move a Story Forward at scholastic.com/BFBresources.

In each visit, you will notice more and more. But this process is not a treasure hunt—you are not taking a stack of books and a ledger sheet and keeping a tally of which book(s) offer the most connections to curriculum or standards. We do not develop strong, lasting bonds of friendship by going to social functions in search of people who can serve our purposes in life. Rather, we live our lives and people cross our paths. We find some of them engaging, intriguing, and fascinating. We come to know them over time. We develop a true friendship and build trust and caring.

A Best Friend Book has sufficient substance and depth to hold up to many visits across the year. A good BFB creates a solid foundation for other work in the classroom community or curriculum. These books are selected because each time you return to a Best Friend Book, you may find yet another point of entry and you leave with new or deeper insight. While there are numerous books with tremendous potential for extension or engagement, a Best Friend Book is one that invites self-reflection and can be revisited to explore language, life, and/or content area insights.

Ultimately, we want Best Friend Books to live in the minds and hearts of each reader-writer in the classroom. We want students to be able to call upon these titles when they are navigating their way through another text as a reader or when constructing a text as a writer. When conferring with a student (or when students are conferring with a peer), these Best Friend Books are also present and waiting to join in the conversation and offer insight.

A Best Friend Book is one that can transform our reading and writing as we revisit it multiple times across the year. Each visit would offer a new reason to think about the book and give students a new understanding of the potential of literature. The familiarity they'll develop will build insights that will become touchstones for your conferring work in reading and writing workshops.

Throughout this book, we will look at the ways in which we can use Best Friend Books with our children to get the most out of the read-aloud experience and create deep connections.

WHAT THE RESEARCH SAYS

Every time we enter a text as a reader, we receive a writing lesson: how to spell, punctuate, use proper grammar, structure a sentence or paragraph, and organize a text. We also learn the many purposes writing serves and the different genres and formats it assumes to serve these varied purposes. (Duke, 2014; Krashen, 2004)

Spotlight on Lester Videos

In my work in schools, staff development workshops, and conferences around the country, I focus on the art and function of reading aloud. I am frequently asked if I have made any videos that illustrate the techniques and joys of the read-aloud. Throughout this book, you will see places where you can stop and review a video demonstration of my work with several different read-alouds as well as more information about using Best Friend Books. In each of these videos, I think aloud to let you see what I consider as I make decisions about how I will use my voice in the read-aloud. I have selected four spreads to read aloud from each of the books to demonstrate the significance of tone, pacing, intensity, and mood. My hope is that *The Ultimate Read-Aloud Resource* will provide you with new options, new energy, and a new commitment to the art of the read-aloud and to the tremendous potential that it holds for your students.

SPOTLIGHT ON LESTER VIDEOS
scholastic.com/BFBresources

BFB Home Visits

Best friends often come home with you for a visit. When they do, you introduce them to your family, explore the things you have in common, and learn even more about each other. Now imagine bringing a Best Friend Book along for a home visit. Because these books are familiar to everyone in the classroom community, every student will have specific insights about each title. The characters will have been the topic of many discussions and may have filtered into the conversations at home already. Let parents/caregivers know that you are introducing a small set of books to the class as Best Friend Books. Explain what that means and how this is different from your typical read-aloud books. You'll find a sample letter to parents in the BFB Home Visits section on scholastic.com/BFBresources. You'll also find materials to help students introduce these books to their families and then read them together. The goal here is to bring a familiar character home for a visit to extend the conversations, insights, and connections. The conversations from school will most certainly spill over into the talk at home, and the conversations from home hold the potential to bring new dimensions to the conversations at school. Check out all of the materials and videos related to BFB Home Visits by looking for the icon throughout the book.

HOME VISIT
scholastic.com/BFBresources

Who Should Read This Book?

As I wrote this book, I thought of all the adults who work with children and have the opportunity to read aloud to them. I thought of the children whose faces grow intense with engagement when the tension rises in a good story and whose smiles break open into a thousand bits of laughter in the funny parts. I wrote as if I were talking to the educators I work with around the country almost every week of the year. When I provide staff development or speak at a conference, I am always aware that among the folks sitting in the audience there will be classroom teachers, Title I teachers, literacy coaches, staff developers, librarians/media specialists, principals, and other administrators—I wrote for them. I wrote knowing that every decision we make must be measured by the answer to one question—"Will this be good for children?" I hope as you read you will be able to say "YES!" when you are thinking about whether you should make read-aloud an essential, nonnegotiable part of every single day for every single child.

Teachers

Clearly, you are the front line in the work of leading children to fall in love with language and literature as they become readers and writers. You are the ones who select the books, who set the tone of the experience, who lure children into a web of texts of all kinds. As teachers, you are the daily dose of read-aloud. Your voices are the ones that linger in the minds of children as they romp around on the playground, stand in line for lunch, or load onto the bus and head for home at the end of the day. You are the ones who introduce new topics and revisit favorite authors and illustrators or bring in new ones. You are the ones who deepen children's understanding of genre and open the doors to new ways of looking at life and the world around us.

Teachers, as I wrote, I envisioned you surrounded by students, captivating them with nothing more than a Best Friend Book and your voice. *The Ultimate Read-Aloud Resource* is designed to deepen your understandings of the power, purpose, and art of the read-aloud experience in your classroom. The text will offer three intentions for read-aloud, to inspire, to invest, and to instruct, and give you specific suggestions for living out those intentions with each read-aloud experience. In addition, there are specific connections to learning theory and to language/literacy development.

Librarians and Media Specialists

Oh, you lucky people! You get to be with all the books and all the kids. What could be better? *The Ultimate Read-Aloud Resource* offers you a means for promoting read-aloud experiences throughout the school day. The three intentions provide a framework for helping your colleagues organize and present books across the curriculum in careful, thoughtful, and purposeful ways. That gives you one more way to assist teachers in the never-ending effort to connect children and books. The accompanying videos will heighten your attention to the design of a book and the signals the book contains to guide your use of tone, intensity, pacing, and mood when you read aloud in the library or in a classroom.

Literacy Coaches and Staff Developers

In your role, you have the opportunity to promote read-aloud experiences as essential instructional intentions. But as you know, talking about it, giving all the reasons for doing more, and even providing the books don't always make it the most effective experience. *The Ultimate Read-Aloud Resource* explains how to gather a study group in a close examination of the art of reading aloud. The text and videos will assist you in coaching your colleagues through the selection of Best Friend Books, articulating the intention for each read-aloud experience, and attending to the specific signals in the text. You'll have the opportunity to move through old favorites and new titles with new insights, bringing the life of the text to the surface through attention to tone, intensity, pacing, and mood.

Principals and Other Administrators

The Ultimate Read-Aloud Resource can deepen your insights into the values of read-aloud in a time when there is greater attention to accountability. Use this tool to justify time spent reading aloud to children in the classrooms of your building. Use this tool to recognize the qualities of an artful, intentional, and meaningful read-aloud.

CHAPTER 1

Why Read-Aloud Matters

"Reading aloud with children is known to be the single most important activity for building the knowledge and skills they will eventually require for learning to read."

—MARILYN JAGER ADAMS, READING RESEARCHER

Perhaps the first hurdle in the teaching of reading is to build the love of books and stories and information. We live in a world of instant access—all we have to do is tap a screen or speak a question into our phones and an answer will follow. Not so long ago, I was working in San Antonio, Texas, and had an afternoon free. As I was strolling along the Riverwalk, I passed a young couple with two small children. The infant was tucked in a sling one parent wore like a kangaroo pouch, and the toddler was buckled into a stroller being pushed by the other parent. What struck me about this little family was that the parents were chatting away, the infant appeared to be sleeping, and the toddler was busily engaged with an iPad. The four of them were strolling amidst an array of birds and insects and trees and flowers and music and aromas and boats and water and food and laughter and people. The toddler never looked up. She didn't point to anything and ask about it. The parents didn't stop and kneel down next to her to point out and name all the interesting things that could have broadened the child's repertoire of sights and sounds and smells and words. Oh, the words they could have used. I ached over the missed opportunities to connect the real world to vocabulary.

A little further down the path, I took a seat at a small table on the sidewalk and ordered a drink and a bite to eat. I watched people with children and wondered what stories they would tell next week when they went back to their regular lives, when the Riverwalk was just a memory. I wondered what bits of their trip would filter into their talk, and what new language and concepts would be lifted to connect with books they may read. I sat there and I wondered.

I hear the demands to raise scores in our schools. I see the impact of the pressure to get more done in less time to meet standards. And I wonder. I wonder what we lose when we let go of those small moments when we kneel down next to a child and look at the world from their level. Where is the fascination with a ladybug strolling across a leaf or an inchworm arcing and stretching its way up a stem? Where are those moments when a child giggles with excitement at the flutter of wings and the sudden flight of a bird? Will we lose the intense natural interest children bring to the worlds of their imagination? Those experiences, it seems to me, are the building blocks of story. The shared experiences, the new discoveries, the fresh new words that tickle a little one's tongue; those are the building blocks of story. In our rush to raise scores, to cover more in less time, we cannot lose sight of the notion that we are raising humans, young and impressionable humans. With that said, let's remind ourselves of the need for play and exploration. Let's remind ourselves of the power of pretend and imagination. Let's remind ourselves that story is a way we recall experience and construct meaning and negotiate our ideas and open a world of new possibilities. The curriculum we once crafted for our first graders, we now deliver to kindergarten children. What's more, in some schools, we ask children as young as six to choose the college they plan to attend once they graduate from high school. This seems a tall order for young children who often don't fully understand what college is (Pappano, 2015). Why all the rush to move children into adulthood? I wonder.

SPOTLIGHT ON LESTER VIDEO

Lester Answers Some Common Questions About Read-Alouds

scholastic.com/BFBresources

How I Was Introduced to the Read-Aloud

What comes to mind when you hear someone talking about the read-aloud? Do you flash back to your own school days and see yourself settling into your desk right after lunch? Is your head resting on your folded arms? Do you hear your teacher's voice recounting the last few events of the pages read aloud yesterday? Maybe your mind takes you to the library, that palace of books where the librarian gathered you and others near enough to get swept away in the current of language flowing on the human voice. Perhaps it isn't a school memory at all. Perhaps you are taken back even further, back to your earliest childhood memories. Does talk of read-aloud evoke the smell of your mother, the tender voice of your grandmother, or the secure feeling of snuggling in close to your father? Is it a particular story or poem you recall, or is it the sound of a voice? Is it the words of the story or the cadence and the rhythm of the language? Is it the reading or the undivided attention showered upon you in those magical moments? What is it about read-aloud experiences that can leave such lasting and powerful memories long after the book is closed…
long after…?

Lester, at a young age, beginning his lifelong love of books and the read-aloud.

My earliest memories of read-aloud take me back to an apartment over the garage behind my Grandmother Thompson's house in Heflin, Alabama. I was four years old. My brother Scott was six, already in school and already reading. I remember these little boxes that came in the mail from time to time. Each box held two books, and those became instant favorites. Each night I took my perch on the wide arm of an overstuffed chair. My brother sat nestled in the seat next to Mother with the book spread across their laps. His slender fingers trailed across the page as that music—released from his mouth—lingered in the air. I basked in the glory of the rhythm, I lusted after that magic, and I coveted the nest where complete adoration flowed from mother to son. I was addicted to the whole idea of it. Of course there were others who read aloud to me. But none had the same impact in my most formative years.

But the most lasting impression of read-aloud was etched into my memory in the library of Cleburne County Elementary School in Heflin, Alabama. The year was 1964. I was eight years old, and our third-grade class made weekly visits to the library on Thursdays. I looked forward to those visits with unwrapping-a-birthday-present eagerness. I longed for Thursday, though not primarily for the opportunity to roam around the

"As we share the words and pictures, the ideas and viewpoints, the rhythms and rhymes, the pain and comfort, and the hopes and fears and big issues of life that we encounter together in the pages of a book, we connect through minds and hearts with our children and bond closely in a secret society associated with the books we have shared. The fire of literacy is created by the emotional sparks between a child, a book, and the person reading."

—MEM FOX

stacks of old books standing at attention, spine-to-spine with new ones. I longed for Thursday for the gift of Mrs. Hand's voice, that slow, deliberate, carefully delivered voice of books. Mrs. Hand had a distinctive voice. Low and resonant like a cello. Smooth and lush like expensive velvet. Slow and unhurried like pouring honey on a February morning. It was as if Mrs. Hand loved one thing more than sharing all those books, only one thing. Us.

When she read, it was clear that she was sharing a treasure, and that this was a most special once-a-week treasure that she held just for us. She had such control over the elements of an artful read-aloud—tone, intensity, pace, and mood. Looking back, I am convinced that my own fascination with the sounds of books read aloud—the very music of the written word played on the instrument of a well-tuned human voice—is grounded in the third-grade memories of our school librarian, Mrs. Hand, sharing her love of books, words, and us in half-hour installments once each week.

Mrs. Hand was charged with such important duties as teaching us to use the card catalog, leading us to pledge our allegiance to the Dewey decimal system, and helping us to become adept at locating the books we needed. Although she was the undisputed queen of that palace of books, she had a deep and abiding love for reading and, more important for us, for the children of our tiny community tucked away in rural Alabama. It was that love that guided her in the application of her knowledge. She was a wise woman, and she understood something essential about becoming literate, something so obvious, yet so rare in the daily practice of our schools. Mrs. Hand understood that mastering the Dewey decimal system, becoming an ace navigator of the card catalog, and developing the ability to locate any title in less than 60 seconds would be useless skills unless we first fell in love with books. She understood that *function* precedes *form*, that the *need to know* drives learning *how to do*, that *passion* for anything is a most powerful driving force in the life of any human being.

Mrs. Hand was not wasting time reading *The Boxcar Children* aloud to our class. She didn't read those weekly installments because she had nothing else planned or because she had planned too little to fill up the time and keep us focused. She didn't read to us because she was too lazy to get off the stool. She didn't read to us because she was too unprofessional to teach us those important tools and skills of library life. She read aloud to us to woo us in, to seduce our

"The unique language of books and literacy is learned the way any language is learned—by using and living it as a way of life."

—JOHN SHEFELBINE

minds and souls into the spell of reading. Like the call of the sirens from ancient Greece, she read to us artfully and with great intention. Mrs. Hand knew what she was doing. She *read aloud* to us deliberately. She selected books specifically for us, books she *knew we'd fall in love with*. She knew that once Henry and Jesse and Violet and precious little Benny found that old, abandoned boxcar, we'd be utterly and hopelessly in love. And she was right. As she read, I pictured myself romping through the pine thickets around our house and stumbling upon a boxcar. I so longed to be Henry, that brave and strong big brother who took charge and made sure all his siblings were cared for. But the truth is that I more closely identified with Benny. I was the younger brother, the weaker one, the sweet and naïve one. And when Benny found that cherished pink cup with the chip in the rim, the one his sisters scoured with a bit of soap and sand, I could taste the cold milk he drank from it. I could feel the chip as the rim touched my lips. And that was my first experience with becoming lost inside a book, falling in with and *living* alongside the characters. I was *forever changed* as a reader. And today, I am convinced it was in that moment that *I was born as a writer*.

WHAT THE RESEARCH SAYS

Reading has cognitive consequences that extend beyond its immediate task of lifting meaning from a particular passage. Furthermore, these consequences are reciprocal and exponential in nature. Accumulated over time— spiraling either upward or downward—they carry profound implications for the development of a wide range of cognitive capabilities. (Cunningham & Zibulsky, 2013; Nell Duke, et al., 2011)

The Seven Functions of Language

Michael Halliday (1973) identified the following seven functions of language that may help fine-tune our thinking about making our read-aloud experiences intentional. Language serves multiple purposes; indeed, because language is functional, it's relatively easy for young children to learn their mother tongue. They quickly learn that they can get their needs met and interact with others in fulfilling ways by using language. Keeping these language functions in mind as you share books with your students may extend the learning possibilities:

INSTRUMENTAL Language for getting things done, for satisfying one's needs

REGULATORY Language for controlling the behavior of others

INTERACTIONAL Language for maintaining and establishing relationships

PERSONAL Language for expressing personality and individuality

HEURISTIC Language for finding things out, for exploring the environment

IMAGINATIVE Language as a means of creating a world of one's own

REPRESENTATIONAL Language for conveying information

Let's take a moment to examine each of these functions as they may relate to our intentions for reading aloud to inspire our students as readers and writers. You can find a printable graphic organizer for The Seven Functions of Language at scholastic.com/BFBresources.

Instrumental Language

The language for getting things done—instrumental—can be heard in numerous read-aloud experiences. We are witnesses to the use of instrumental language when a writer uses language that enables a character to accomplish his or her desires and needs. If we select books thoughtfully, our students will hear the way characters use language to meet their needs, accomplish their goals, and make their wishes known each time we read aloud. As a result, we broaden our students' understandings of the potentials of both spoken and written language. Consider Max in *Bunny Cakes* (Wells, 1997). He needed "red-hot marshmallow squirters" for his earthworm cake, so he added that to the list Ruby gave him to take to the grocer. Max knows the power of language to get things done, even though he is learning to control written language. We see another example in the comments from the hens in *Three Hens and a Peacock* (Laminack, 2011) when they are planning what to wear for their day by the road stopping cars.

Regulatory Language

By attempting to control the behavior of others—evident in the notes and signs and warnings sprinkled throughout a book—we are using regulatory language. These may be sent by one character to another or encountered by a character in the plot of a story. Regulatory language may be sprinkled into the art as signs or labels or captions. Examples of regulatory language may also be seen in the speech of one character giving direction to another, as in *Saturdays and Teacakes* (Laminack, 2004): "My mother always said, '*You stop and look both ways when you get to Chandler's. I don't care if the light is green. I'll hear about it if you don't.*'" We can also call attention to the use of regulatory language in situations where one character is trying to be in control. Consider *The Recess Queen* (O'Neill, 2002), when Mean Jean says, "'Say WHAT?' Mean Jean growled. 'Say WHO?' Mean Jean howled. 'Say YOU! Just who do you think you're talking to?'" These examples demonstrate for our students that language can be used to control the behaviors of others.

Interactional Language

Interactional language is used to maintain and establish relationships. We can demonstrate the function of interactional language through a read-aloud of *A Letter to Amy* (Keats, 1998). Peter's letter to Amy extending an invitation to his birthday party is a clear example of written language intended to maintain a friendship. Other examples can be found in the delightful books of Alma Flor Ada, *Dear Peter Rabbit* (2006), *Yours Truly, Goldilocks* (2001), and *With Love, Little Red Hen* (2004), in which letters are sent between the characters of our favorite stories from childhood. In addition, you may find it helpful to point out incidences in other favorite read-alouds where characters are using dialogue to begin or continue friendships. Each of these will be yet another demonstration of the many ways we use both oral and written language.

Personal Language

Personal language—used to express personality or individuality—can be found in most any read-aloud in which the writer reveals a character through playful word choice. Junie B. Jones, the spirited young character featured by Barbara Parks in numerous books, comes to mind as a good example of a character whose language is part of her personality. You will find similar examples in the Amelia Bedelia books created by Peggy Parish. For other examples of personal language, share Helen Lester's *Hooway for Wodney Wat*, or Roald Dahl's *The BFG*, or Judy Blume's books featuring the effervescent younger brother, Fudge. In each case, the writer's choice of language for these characters etches a lasting memory in the mind of the reader and listener.

WHAT THE RESEARCH SAYS

"One of the most important and challenging tasks that young children encounter when they begin their formal schooling is listening to directions, and children who can make sense of the requests or directives they receive are likely to fare better than students who need more time to decipher a sentence and determine the meaning of an unfamiliar word." (Cunningham, A. & Zibulsky, J., 2014, pp. 21–22)

Heuristic Language

Heuristic language, used for finding things out or for exploring the environment, is quite common in classrooms. Heuristic language can be heard in the hundreds of questions asked each day in a typical classroom. We can also see it in the all-about and how-to books and the information books in our nonfiction collections. We can feature this use of language through read-aloud experiences with selections from Gail Gibbons, Cathryn Sill, Seymour Simon, Diane Siebert, Nicola Davies, and Thomas Locker. Many of our favorite nonfiction writers will give us ample opportunity to use language to find out and explore.

> "No wonder experts tell us that children need to hear a thousand stories read aloud before they begin to learn to read for themselves. A thousand! That sounds daunting. But when we do the sums, it isn't as bad as we might think. Three stories a day will deliver us a thousand stories in one year alone, let alone in the four or five years prior to school."
>
> —MEM FOX

WHAT THE RESEARCH SAYS

It's not surprising to learn that there is a correlation between a child developing oral language skills and the sophistication of the questions she's asked during the read-aloud. Researchers kept track of what parents said to their 27-month-olds while reading aloud to them; sure enough, open-ended questions and sophisticated prompts that sparked further exploration of the book seemed to promote expressive language skills and a more robust vocabulary—evident when these same children were tested again between the ages of 30 and 42 months. Open-ended questions and sophisticated prompts (beyond "yes or no" questions and simple directives such as "turn the page" and "point to the picture") encourage deep reading, deep discussion, deep thinking—and deep learning! (Cunningham & Zibulsky, 2014)

Imaginative Language

The language of the imagination is used to create a world of one's own. Young children seem quite comfortable with pretending and talking about things and situations as if they were real. They create towns with blocks, go grocery shopping in the dramatic play areas of their classrooms, and travel to the moon just by climbing up a ladder. Each time we read aloud a book in which the author takes us on a journey of suspended logic—where we imagine and pretend—we are wallowing in imaginative language. So when the children in *Roxaboxen* (McLerran, 2004) create a town using rocks to outline the buildings, and create their own rules and government and currency, they use imaginative language. They talk about imaginary things as if they were real. Through books such as this we help our students see imaginative language at work. Clearly, then, any work of fantasy, folktale, or fairy tale capable of evoking the imagination can be read aloud, showing yet another function for both written and oral language.

WHAT THE RESEARCH SAYS

"Those who write about the nonfiction/fiction controversy should read more nonfiction, specifically the research showing that reading fiction has a profound impact on language and literacy development, including vocabulary, spelling, and grammar. In a recent study, frequency of voluntary reading of both 'middle-brow' and 'high-brow' fiction was a very strong predictor of vocabulary size. All this makes reading demanding nonfiction texts possible.

Studies also show that fiction exposes readers to other views of the world and other ways of thinking, and increases the ability to deal with uncertainty, which is crucial for problem-solving. Fiction is the bridge between everyday conversational language and academic language." (Stephen Krashen, 2015)

Representational Language

For a striking example of representational language, take a look at *The Handmade Alphabet* by Laura Rankin, in which sign language is demonstrated in beautiful language and art. The National Council of Teachers of English's Orbis Pictus Awards are a good source of outstanding books that convey facts and information. (See www.ncte.org/elem/awards/orbispictus.)

Closing Thoughts

There is no doubt that read-aloud matters. The research is clear, but more important, any adult can bear witness to the power of reading aloud to children. Imagine how that power intensifies when we select a small set of stories that we read again and again. Through repeated visits with a single story, children deepen insights about how story works. Together we discover how writers reveal characters. We uncover the relationships between characters and setting. We explore the impact of setting upon plot. We gain insight into the potentials for secondary characters in the development of the story. We begin to understand how tension is built, and come to recognize the markers of a story arc. We visit this collection of carefully selected books again and again because conceptual development takes time. As we visit and revisit a Best Friend Book, we come back to the book with more language, more insight, better questions, and deeper connections. And once we grasp these essential literary concepts, we can begin to move out to broader experiences and apply those insights in new situations.

CHAPTER 2

Toward the Intentional Read-Aloud

> *"After nearly three decades of gathering first graders around me to read a story, I believe that a wealth of experiences plus a love of reading are the keys to a happy life."*
>
> **—MARIA WALTHER, FIRST-GRADE TEACHER AND AUTHOR**

There was a time when read-aloud was as firmly entrenched in the daily routine of school as going to lunch. Teachers read aloud to their students with the regularity of school bells announcing the beginning of a new day. No one questioned the practice—what could possibly be wrong with something so sensible, so enjoyable, something so thoroughly satisfying as reading aloud to students? Who would dare question the motives of a teacher sitting at the front of a room on a tall stool, holding an open book, while captivating the full attention of an entire classroom of children? And think of it, all this with nothing more than the human voice and well-crafted language.

Yet as I work in schools around the country, teachers report feeling they don't have time for read-aloud in their increasingly busy days. They report feeling they can hardly justify time spent reading to children, and that to do so makes them feel subversive. How very sad that something so pure, something so very simple has become suspect. How very sad that we have reached a point in schooling where as teachers we feel we must justify our every decision, even the most basic, commonsensical decisions about taking time to read aloud to children. So I invite you to join me in an effort to reclaim read-aloud for our students and, yes, even for ourselves. Let's reinvent this tried-and-true practice, this commonsensical standard in the education of our children. Let's reclaim this sensible source of endless *inspiration*. Let's reinvigorate this trusted means of *investing* in the minds of our students and opening their lives to a world beyond their own imaginations. Let's reenvision read-aloud as a respected means of instruction. Let's make every read-aloud *intentional*. Toward that goal, we must be thoughtful in our selection of texts to read aloud. We must be clear in our own minds about *why* we are reading a particular title. I am advocating for reading aloud with the frequency of birdsong and with the zeal of a street performer. I am advocating for reading aloud from a wide array of titles that represent a variety of authors and illustrators and genres and topics.

SPOTLIGHT ON
LESTER VIDEO

What Makes a Read-Aloud Intentional?

scholastic.com/BFBresources

I am advocating for reading aloud several times each day. But I am also advocating that each classroom have a small collection, five titles—Best Friend Books—that are read aloud again and again to build a level of familiarity that one would have with a best friend.

GENERAL READ-ALOUD EXPERIENCES:

- Serve as a foundation of a solid, thoughtful language and literacy program

- Create scaffolds for connecting understanding to independent reading and writing

- Support content in every subject area by building background knowledge that supports inquiry

- Nourish the intellect (listening comprehension is built through daily experiences hearing texts read aloud, participating in discussions of those texts, and making connections with those texts)

- Demonstrate thinking as we and our students share personal connections, make connections to other texts, take in new information, and adjust personal views

- Provide opportunities for deeper reflection that may lead to repeated reading of the same text

- Expand vocabulary and create sensitivity to language

- Provide exposure to text structures, helping our students understand how texts can be organized and noting why specific structures are used

- Provide exposure to a variety of text types and help our students recognize the differences between nonfiction and fiction, poetry and prose

- Provide a demonstration of phrased, fluent reading, showing the function of tone, intensity, pacing, and mood

- Create a literary community in the classroom where a pool of shared meanings and a common language can develop

- Expand children's literary knowledge by developing their understanding of plot, character, themes, and setting

- Build a repertoire of genres, favorite authors, and favorite illustrators

- Expand our students' notions of writer's craft and how craft helps the reader construct meaning

BEST FRIEND BOOK READ-ALOUD EXPERIENCES:

- Build a collection of stories that all students in the classroom community know intimately

- Bring a set of characters into the classroom community that students know the way they know a best friend

- Result in a small collection of books that all students carry in their hearts and in their heads

- Establish a literary knowledge base common to all members of the classroom community

- Establish intimate familiarity with each Best Friend author's writing craft and unique techniques for spinning a winning tale

- Showcase the lovely language—such as surprising turns of phrase, playful and poetic prose, and musical phrasing—unique to each Best Friend author

- Heighten awareness of the ways in which print and graphics work together to enhance meaning and enjoyment

- Invite an "insider's understanding" of the ways in which literature illuminates, expands, and enhances life

- Help establish an emotional connection with particular authors, themes, topics, and genres—and reading!

To make read-aloud *intentional,* I believe that we must be as thoughtful in our planning as we are when selecting manipulatives for mathematics or when establishing the flow of a classroom. We must select the books we will read with the same care we take in designing centers or in setting up a science lab. We must be as diligent in considering our reasons for reading aloud as we are in selecting the focus of a mini-lesson in reading and writing workshops. In short, we must pay careful attention to our *intentions* for the read-aloud.

QUESTIONS TO ASK YOURSELF:

- Why do I read aloud to my students?

- What are my expectations for the experience?

- What result or product do I hope for?

- How will my students be different for living through these experiences with me?

- Am I hoping to motivate them to explore a topic or genre?

- Am I inviting them to meet a new author or illustrator?

- Am I leading them to compare the organizational framework of this story with a favorite known by all?

- Am I simply reading today for some future benefit, investing the time now to connect future instruction later?

- Am I reading to introduce specific vocabulary that will be essential in understanding the concepts for a unit of study in a subject area?

- Am I reading to contrast the multiple meanings of troublesome words?

- Am I reading to raise awareness of a targeted issue?

- Am I reading to model a specific reading strategy or skill?

- Am I reading to draw them in, to lure them into wanting to read more for themselves?

- Am I reading to bank images and language we will draw upon in an upcoming study?

As I see it, all these *intentions* can be easily grouped under three broad reasons for reading aloud. We make read-aloud intentional when we purposely select texts and times with the intent to *inspire, invest,* or *instruct.*

Reading Aloud to Inspire

Mrs. Hand read to my third-grade class with no other obvious intention than to captivate our hearts. She was reading to *inspire* new devotees. She wanted us to love reading, to lust after language, to crave time with books. Mrs. Hand knew we had to fall in love before we would ever see the need for strategies and skills that would give us the stamina to live through a chapter book independently. Remember, Mrs. Hand understood some essentials about learning. Let me quickly remind you—she understood that *function* precedes *form*, that the *need to know* drives learning *how to do*, that *passion* for anything is a most powerful driving force in the life of any human being. In other words, if we teach them *how* without teaching them *why*, we leave them in a situation where they don't know *when*. Knowing how to do something without knowing why you do it leaves you at a loss about *when* that new learning is needed.

Think about the teenagers you have known. One very common passion driving them, virtually *all* of them, is the vision of driving a vehicle. How is it that young people can become so enamored with the ability to drive? What plants the seed of the notion that driving is something desirable? We live in a very mobile society in which people equate mobility with freedom. From the time children are born, they are on the go. Children are strapped into car seats several times each week as

the caregivers run errands, drive them to and from babysitters, day care, school, after-school events, and more. Children see the ability to drive demonstrated over and over without explicit intentions for making them good drivers. Rather, it is the mobility, the ability to accomplish so many things independently without reliance on someone else, that is the lure. I have met very few teenagers who were not absolutely *lusting* after a driver's license by the time they were 14 years old. And remember: all they have is the consistent demonstration of the *function* of this ability. Their experience with drivers is an ever-present demonstration of all the freedom this *skill* and *ability* brings with it. It takes no cajoling, no bribes, no points or pizzas. It takes little more than being witness in daily life to the *function* of the act itself.

So what can we do to create that same lusting after language, books, reading?

Perhaps it is as simple as driving. We demonstrate by our daily actions the essential *functions* of reading in the life of a human being. The point here is that read-aloud experiences can be thoughtfully planned to demonstrate the functions of language to inspire our students to read and write. So each time we read aloud, we demonstrate that language has purpose and power. We demonstrate that as readers and writers we strengthen our ability to use language each time we read or listen to someone else read. We put that growing strength to use each time we write and speak. As teachers, we have both the insight and the knowledge to select books carefully, thoughtfully, and purposefully. As teachers, we can decide what to feature or draw attention to as we read aloud. As teachers, we can lead our students to understand and appreciate the potentials of language that can inspire them to be readers and writers themselves. One way we do that is by being keenly aware of the functions or purposes that language serves in our lives and making those more visible for our students. And when we revisit a Best Friend Book again and again, we have the time to slow down, to look closely at a single element and notice how writers lay the groundwork for our work as readers.

WHAT THE RESEARCH SAYS

Researchers suggest that the most valuable aspect of the read-aloud activity is that it gives children experience with decontextualized language, requiring them to make sense of ideas that are about something beyond the here and now. (Beck & Sandora, 2016; Beck & McKeown, 2001)

Reading Aloud to Develop Language and Concepts

When we *invest* in anything, we expect to make small installments over long periods of time with the understanding that dividends will not be collected until much later. Talk with anyone nearing retirement and they will tell you how very important it is to make contributions of any size as often as possible to the general fund. Retirement age is too late to begin thinking about what we *could* have done or *might* have done or *should* have done to live well in our later years.

Likewise, if *investment* is the specific intention of a read-aloud, then we select books for the potential each of them holds. We think in advance of the outcome or product we desire. So with that in mind, we begin with a close look at the specific subject and the unit of study. We identify the core understandings needed for successful completion and select books that will enable us to create scaffolds through exposure to images, specific vocabulary, and concepts that new learning can be built upon. We sequence these texts both in a way that will be logical for the learners and will scaffold the concepts in the study.

Then, in careful, thoughtfully planned, and patient installments we layer each read-aloud to establish a collective common ground of the classroom community, and we pace the presentation of texts to the ability of our students to process the essential information. The main point here is to *invest* the time *now* to read

"Reading aloud is not a cure-all. Not quite. But it is such a wonderful antidote for turning on turned-off readers and brightening up dull writing that I feel it's worthwhile to plead again for its regular occurrence in every classroom, not only those classrooms at the younger end of school.... The value of my writing increases before my very eye, beneath my very pen. The investment in listening, I have found, pays dividends."

—MEM FOX

aloud from these specifically selected texts with the expressed intention that the time spent now will yield significant dividends during the actual study as it unfolds. Think of it this way: time spent reading aloud on this end helps to establish the common ground that you connect with comfortably as you begin the more in-depth work of the unit of study. For a detailed listing of books carefully selected to support read-alouds intended to invest time, language, and concepts, see *Learning Under the Influence of Language and Literature* (Laminack and Wadsworth, 2006) and *Reading Aloud Across the Curriculum* (Laminack & Wadsworth, 2006).

Reading Aloud to Instruct

When we set out to instruct another person, there is typically a relationship established that defines our role. The instructor is assumed to be competent, masterful, accomplished, and perhaps even artful in something that the apprentice or student *needs* or *wants* to learn. But as teachers, our work is done in an institution of learning where student attendance is mandatory. Our students are not seeking us out because of our passion and competence, or because of our accomplishments or our artful application of knowledge and skill. Our students aren't even selecting to be in our specific classrooms. Their choices are limited from the start. It isn't their drive to know, their passion for a topic, that sends them out on a mission to find a mentor. So we can't assume that all of our students are eager to learn what we have been charged to teach.

Let's explore how a read-aloud intended to instruct can be a most beneficial experience in this situation. Assume for a moment that your students are expected to study story elements in language arts. Let's further assume that the curriculum expects your students to be able to compare and contrast two different ways a writer uses dialogue.

SPOTLIGHT ON
LESTER VIDEO

What Makes a Read-Aloud Instructional?

scholastic.com/BFBresources

One way this might be approached is through traditional lessons from language arts textbooks, follow-up exercises, and a homework assignment. Clearly, most teachers are adept at extending these more traditional approaches with interesting options that make the work more engaging. However, vocabulary and background knowledge may be uneven. Some may read the textbook and gather information they simply transfer to a worksheet or exercise, while others see the examples and are able to apply the information to classroom lessons almost immediately. It would be quite possible, then, for students in both these situations to "do well" on the assignment without developing any deeper understanding of how to transfer the information into their own writing work.

If we follow Frank Smith's idea that learning is natural, that we learn from the company we keep, then what does that suggest for us about reading aloud with intentions to instruct? Can we actually read aloud as instruction? Yes, we can.

The key, as I see it, lies in our intentions. If we intend to instruct through the read-aloud experience, then much rests on the sense of community we have established and on the very careful selection of books. As with any intentional instruction, we must know what we expect our students to learn as a result of the experience. We begin with those expectations, and we place them alongside our knowledge of our students. We assess their existing background knowledge, including their current insights and misunderstandings. Through initial conversations, we determine their facility with vocabulary related to the topic and their ability to speak with specificity using that vocabulary. These insights aid us in selecting books to read aloud and also serve as common ground for developing and extending communal concepts about this topic.

So, with the example above, we would select two titles from our Best Friend Books where the authors use dialogue for different purposes. For example, dialogue in one book may be used to give us insight into the character's thoughts. Yet, in another book, it is to give the main character a scaffold to reveal the tension in the plot. Revisiting two familiar books puts us in a position where we can turn to a specific scene and point out explicitly how dialogue is being used.

Closing Thoughts

Reading aloud can be a powerful tool in our instruction. Literature in the hands of a skillful teacher can be focused to inspire or invest or instruct. Clearly, a single book could be read once to fulfill any one of these intentions and then returned to the classroom library for students to read independently. But the books we think of as Best Friend Books, that small collection of carefully selected titles we will revisit again and again, are ripe with potential for all three of these intentions. It is easy to imagine the first read, a nonstop, start-to-finish "movie read," presented with the intention of inspiring students to explore that particular title, other titles by the same author, other titles in the same genre, or ones that share the same theme. But that same Best Friend Book can be revisited on another day with a focus on how the writer reveals the character because your intention is to invest read-aloud experiences in developing that idea across two or more titles. And, of course, that same title could be revisited during a mini-lesson when you explore a single scene or one small segment of print to instruct your students on a specific teaching point.

CHAPTER 3

Selecting and Using Best Friend Books

"*Neither poverty nor a thousand misfortunes should deprive any child of a book, because books DO change lives. They did mine.*"

—F. ISABEL CAMPOY, PROFESSOR AND POET

It seems quite simple, really. If we want children to *desire* the ability to read well, we *inspire* them by inviting them in. We read to them, showing our sheer delight in the act of reading. We read to them, letting them hear the sound effects in the background of our minds, the voices of the characters lifting up off the pages, the very mood of the text in the tone and intensity of our voices. We control the most basic elements of a read-aloud with our human voice—tone, pacing, intensity, and mood. We let our children live alongside characters in books. We let them investigate the habitats of polar bears and explore hot, dry desert terrain. We let them stand alongside children facing bigotry in the Jim Crow South. We let them know the sting of bullies. We let them know the strength of standing tall and facing a challenge. We take them into the celebrations of another culture. We let them laugh with delight at the antics of a favorite character. We show them two perspectives on the same news event. We lead a great discussion as a reaction to a letter to the editor. We launch a new study from the questions raised by responses to a book on bats. We read to them. We *read aloud to them*, and we do so with carefully thought-out *intentions*. We let them see, experience, live through the freedoms and thrills and satisfaction a reading life can provide.

When we read aloud to inspire, our expectations of students are simple and direct. We want nothing more than to pique their interest, to spark a desire, to entice them to read. Our ultimate goal is that they fall in love with language and books; that they lust after language and books and reading as they will later lust after driving. Therefore, any intentional read-aloud designed to inspire would not ask students to answer a set of questions, give a retelling, unpack meaning, host a conversation, define vocabulary, write a character sketch, or compare or contrast anything. None of that would follow a read-aloud to inspire our students. Rather, we want to leave them laughing. We want to see their eyes welling up with tears in those poignant moments in the text. We want them holding their breath as suspense builds. We want to leave them begging: "One more book . . . ," "Five more pages . . . ," "Just one more paragraph, please, we have to know what happens. . . ." We want them talking about the book as they are walking to lunch, and when scurrying about on the playground or boarding the bus. We want the language lingering in their heads. We want the reading to have lasting power. We want them to want reading for themselves.

So when we read aloud with the intention to inspire, we will naturally rely on favorite authors and beloved titles that we have fallen in love with over and over. One thing is sure here: our passion and zeal for the act of reading and for the language being read must be evident. Then we move on to introduce our students to new authors and illustrators, broadening the set of options, widening the net for matchmaking, so to speak. We are careful to introduce new genres and expose our students to a range of themes, styles, and topics. We select material for read-aloud experiences knowing that our students have varied interests and backgrounds that will influence their attractions to reading. When reading aloud with the intention to inspire, we may select a short poem about a baseball game, a feature article about changes at the park, or a letter to the editor protesting a plan

> "It is not enough to simply teach children to read; we have to give them something worth reading. Something that will stretch their imaginations—something that will help them make sense of their own lives and encourage them to reach out toward people whose lives are quite different from their own."
>
> —KATHERINE PATERSON

to clear the woods behind the school to make a space for a fast-food restaurant. We may select a chapter book that will be shared in several installments across two weeks. We may select student-authored material or perhaps something we have written. We may select a collection of riddles and jokes. We may select a set of stories about school. The point is, we select *what* we read with the same intentionality we follow in selecting *why* we read. In fact, *what* we read aloud is inextricably connected to *why* we read aloud.

What Are the Qualities of Best Friend Books?

We all have favorite books that we love to share with students. But a Best Friend Book is more than just a favorite read-aloud. As teachers, we each have books that we read to our students for the sheer joy of it. We have others we use to introduce a topic or launch a unit of study. Those are wonderful tools for our teaching and serve an important purpose in our students' development. However, a Best Friend Book is something more. We choose a BFB because it has depth and breadth that enables us to return over and over as we unearth the nuances of meaning, the subtleties in language, the layers of characters and their motivations, and more.

A BFB is a trusted text that we carry in our hearts and heads as we move about the room from writer to reader conferring about an array of topics from developing a character to interpreting a text. It is more than a read-aloud to spark interest in memoir or launch a study of realistic fiction. It is more than an excellent text to explore how transitions work to move the reader from scene to scene. It is more than the best example of how to use dialogue. It is a rich, robust, deep text that allows us to see more each time we visit, to gain deeper insights, and to come away knowing more about ourselves as readers and writers.

SPOTLIGHT ON
LESTER VIDEO

**What Are the Qualities
of a Best Friend Book?**

scholastic.com/BFBresources

Creating a Classroom Collection of Best Friend Books

When all the members of the classroom share deep and intimate knowledge of a small collection of books, a new level of communication about reading and writing becomes possible. For example, if everyone in the class is very familiar with the book *Apt. 3* by Ezra Jack Keats, I can refer them to a particular scene where the hall light is broken. If in one of our visits we reread that scene and delve into the reasons Keats may have included that detail, we will have a deeper understanding of the use of specific detail. Following that epiphany, I will be able to sit next to any young writer in the class and ask, "So where is your 'hall light' detail in this piece?" and every writer in the room will know what I mean.

Visiting a small collection of Best Friend Books many times allows us to delve into small details during each visit, resulting in deeper insights than we will have with other books in our classroom library. We can discuss how an author most effectively reveals the characters and point to examples. We can identify where the tension builds and talk about how the author makes that happen. Our BFBs will be the books we carry in our hearts and in our heads each time we engage in a conversation about our reading or writing. Our insights about these books become a reading lens for us as we approach new texts and a writing lens for us to plan our own writing. BFBs become a part of us; we carry them with us as we move through the grades.

> *When all the members of the classroom share deep and intimate knowledge of a small collection of books, a new level of communication about reading and writing becomes possible.*

Possibilities for Grouping Read-Aloud and Best Friend Books

When we gather books for reading aloud to invest time, language, and conceptual information, we may group them around the following:

AUTHOR STUDY. A collection of books written by one author selected for a close examination of the writer's style.

GENRE. A collection of books from the same genre selected to explore the parameters of the genre. This may lead into a unit of study in writing or reading workshops.

TEXT STRUCTURE. A collection of books selected to demonstrate one or more ways of organizing texts or to demonstrate selected craft techniques in writing.

TOPIC. A collection of books selected to establish background, build vocabulary, develop concepts, or otherwise create a framework for deeper study of a specific topic, such as the Underground Railroad, the water cycle, or bats.

THEME. A collection of books selected to broaden or deepen an understanding of a selected theme, such as friendship, community, bullying, and so on.

We recommend five titles for a collection of Best Friend Books. You can find printable graphic organizers for Possibilities for Grouping Read-Aloud and Best Friend Books and Guiding Questions for Selecting Best Friend Books at scholastic.com/BFBresources. Guiding questions for selecting titles include:

- Does this book have adequate depth and substance to warrant visiting again and again?

- Do the language and art offer various lenses for several visits?

- Are the literary elements strong enough to support focused exploration?

- Will this book serve as a lens for thinking about reading other books?

- Will this book help build reading insights that can be "flipped" into writing opportunities? See *Writers ARE Readers* (Laminack and Wadsworth, 2015).

SPOTLIGHT ON
LESTER VIDEO

**How Do You Build a
Powerful BFB Collection?**

scholastic.com/BFBresources

Why Limit Best Friend Collections to Five Books?

Read-aloud experiences are essential in the development of readers and writers. There is no limit to the number of books, stories, poems, articles, and other texts that I'd recommend for typical read-aloud experiences across the day. However, the idea behind selecting a small collection of books designated as Best Friend Books moves beyond the typical read-aloud in both intention and exposure. Since the intention with BFBs is to become intimately familiar with each book, the number of books has to be small. I believe five is sufficient without becoming a burden. Remember, the intention is that these five books will live in the hearts and minds of each student in the classroom community. We are working to develop a level of familiarity that enables us to carry these books with us into our reading and writing lives, to call upon them as trusted mentors, and to tag them as we confer with one another across the year. Each of the five will be introduced via the uninterrupted "movie read" and will then be revisited several more times across the year. I find it is unrealistic to expect students (or teachers) to be that intimately familiar with more than five picture books.

WHAT THE RESEARCH SAYS

When it comes to genre, form follows function. As Nell Duke and her co-authors remind us (2012), "Every text is meant to do something for someone—an advertisement to convince us to buy something, a nutrition label to tell us what a food product contains....Today, many scholars see genres primarily as defined by their purposes"—what is the primary aim of the text? What is it trying to accomplish? Answering those questions will help us understand why the writing appears in a particular form or format. (Nell Duke, et al., 2012)

Assigning Best Friend Books
to Specific Grade Levels

When selecting the titles for a BFB collection, I am conscious of the substance of the book. That is, I want to make sure each title has layers we can peel back as we visit it again and again over time. But I also want to connect with the emotional and developmental range of students. I have taken books with me into classrooms knowing the story would make a great read-aloud only to discover that I needed to move it up to use with an older group if I wanted to read it again the next day and go deeper. As you read, make note of what you believe you'd like to lead students to notice and think about. Chances are that your first reading or two will fill a couple of pages in your notebook. After those initial readings, take a moment to review your notes and cluster what you have noticed:

- character(s)

- setting

- challenge or problem

- attempts to reach a solution

- solution

- craft in language

- structure

Then reread with only one of those in mind. For example, as you read a third time, think about the main character (MC) only. Notice how the MC is revealed. Is it through dialogue or action? Is it through what others say about the MC? Is it through how the MC reacts to problems or opportunities? Is it through interior monologue or through what other characters are thinking? Do the actions and comments of other characters serve as a window into the MC? As you read with the MC as your focus, think about how you'd describe that character. Think about appearance and demeanor, and mannerisms and behaviors. As you think about the type of person the MC is, consider these two questions:

1) What is your evidence?

2) How did the writer and/or illustrator reveal this?

Now you'll have a deeper understanding of character development. That insight creates a framework for you to lead your students to do the same as you read and revisit books in your BFB set.

Finding the best fit involves taking the time to read and reread the book several times, shifting your focus each time. Approaching the story with a new lens each time focuses your thinking and helps you notice nuances you may miss otherwise. Consider repeating the example above with the lens focused on a secondary character, or zooming in on how tension is built in the plot, or thinking carefully about how the setting is integrated into the story. You can find a printable graphic organizer for Assigning Best Friend Books to Specific Grade Levels at scholastic.com/BFBresources.

WHAT THE RESEARCH SAYS

The research makes clear that the benefits of rereading are numerous and potent. What do we know about rereading as an instructional strategy? Consider these studies, both golden oldies and current:

- Rereading helps students develop a deeper understanding of what they have read. (Roskos & Neuman, 2014)

- Rereading helps students read with greater fluency, allowing them to give more attention to making sense of what they have read. (Rasinski, 2010)

- Rereading helps students develop greater accuracy in reading. When students reread, words that they may have struggled to decode on a first reading become increasingly easier to parse. (Samuels, 1979)

- Rereading leads to much deeper and more sophisticated discussions and should be a common instructional strategy in every classroom. It's an opportunity for children to understand how text is constructed and the array of decisions every writer must make as he or she uses print to convey a particular set of understandings. Rereading not only builds students' confidence as readers, but also builds their capacity to read deeply, responsibly, and with full joyful engagement. (Beers & Probst, 2012)

Let's explore one other example and consider how we would revisit a story with setting in mind. Let's assume for this example that the story is set in an apartment building in a city and it is a gloomy, rainy day. As we read, let's notice how the rain impacts the story. Does it limit the characters in any way? Does it cause them to stay indoors? Does it affect the mood in the story? Does it have any bearing on the mood of the characters? How is the plot dependent upon it being a rainy day? Would the characters have made other choices in different weather? Would the story have been different if the weather had been mild and sunny or cold and in the middle of a blizzard? How does the placement of characters in an apartment building impact the plot and the characters? Would the story have been different if the same characters lived in a two-story farmhouse in the rolling hills of eastern North Carolina? Does the apartment building offer opportunities that would be unavailable in the suburbs? As you read, tune in to the idea that the writer made conscious choices about every nuance. Each decision has an intended impact.

The point here is to be conscious of what it is you want to unearth in your visits with each BFB. Reading and revisiting a story many times, revisiting each time with a specific lens, making notes of insights and evidence and technique, and then reflecting on what you glean will help you realize the depth of work each book can support. These insights will guide you in deciding which books best fit for the age/grade level.

CAN A BEST FRIEND BOOK "WORK" AT MORE THAN ONE GRADE LEVEL?

Most of us can tell stories of some book or another that somehow became the "exclusive property" of a particular grade level. I recall leading a workshop for a district several years ago. There was an emphasis on moving toward a literature-based model of reading instruction and the conversation shifted to whether a grade level could lay claim to a particular title. There was a great deal of discussion about *Charlotte's Web*, and it became quite clear that in this district, fourth grade had laid claim to the book. Teachers had spent a great deal of time creating files of questions and activities for students to respond to after reading each chapter. There were haystacks to be made from Chinese noodles and melted butterscotch

SPOTLIGHT ON LESTER VIDEO

Best Friend Books and Grade Levels

scholastic.com/BFBresources

chips. There were spider webs to be woven from black yarn and coat hangers. Messages were written on those webs in Elmer's glue and sprinkled with silver glitter. The culminating event was a play performed at night for the parents and community. Needless to say, *Charlotte's Web* was a big deal in fourth grade. From the conversation, it became clear that some second-grade teachers had been reading *Charlotte's Web* aloud to their class. As you might imagine, this was not well received and I was being asked whether it was appropriate. Well… don't ask me unless you want to know what I think!

Here's what I said: Let's just think about this. Currently, *Charlotte's Web* is a cultural event, a rite of passage, and a marker of being in fourth grade. A great deal of time is devoted to that whole event. A *great deal* of time. It appears the concern is that having a second-grade teacher read the book aloud will "ruin" it for all fourth graders. Hold that thought for a moment. Have any of you, as adults, ever read the same book twice? Ever paid money to watch the same movie more than once? Ever stood in line to see the same play a second time? I suspect the answer to that is yes. And I suspect the reason is because the book, movie, or play was so compelling and complex that you simply couldn't take in all of it in one visit. I suspect that the second time through you actually noticed more, tuned in differently, and relished particular moments that you missed the first time. I suspect you needed that first time to provide a context, a road map, that helped you fit all the bits together and to "get" the story. I suspect the second or third visit was when you were able to take in the nuances and understand more deeply, to feel and think and relish the delight of it all.

So let's think about *Charlotte's Web*. It's a beautiful story that holds such meaning for readers. Let's imagine that a second-grade teacher reads it aloud a bit at a time over several days in the classroom. What lingers with the seven- to eight-year-old? Maybe it's the magic of a spider that can write. Maybe it's life on the farm. Maybe it's more. But later, two years later, a fourth grader picks up that book and reads it independently. That fourth grader will read, think, reflect, and loop back in the text. That fourth grader will recall and notice and chuckle at something that may have been misunderstood in second grade. That fourth grader will come to the end of the book and think about friendships and choices. Now fast forward. That same child is now an adult—let's say 47. Now at 47, an old tattered copy of *Charlotte's Web* turns up in the back of a closet. An afternoon is spent sitting with

> *"One cannot read a book: one can only reread it. A good reader, a major reader, an active and creative reader is a rereader."*
>
> **—VLADIMIR NABOKOV**

that old treasure (and maybe a glass of wine). The 47-year-old reaches the last page and sits quietly as tears well up. The 47-year-old says nothing but sits there thinking about the power of unconditional love and marvels at the fact that it had not been noticed all those years ago.

You see, the book never changed. Not one dot on a single "i" has changed on a single page. The reader changed. The reader had life experiences, developed new concepts, misplaced trust, fell in love, lost friends, and simply lived all those years between visits with that book. Each time that reader came back to *Charlotte's Web,* the book sat waiting. Each time that reader came back, the book held the same potential. Each time that reader came back ready for more of what the text always held.

WHAT THE RESEARCH SAYS

The relation each text has to the texts surrounding it is often known as *intertextuality*. Readers build understanding as they draw information from a range of texts. Reading multiple texts across the same theme, topic, genre, or issue automatically fosters close reading and deepens and refines subject knowledge. As noted by renowned literacy researcher Peter Johnston: "To understand a text deeply, we need multiple perspectives. To understand a subject, idea, or concept more deeply, we need multiple texts because each text offers another author's perspective on the subject." (2009)

As readers finish one book in the set, they are better prepared for reading and understanding the next book in the set—and so on. Each book builds on the last. Plus, when students read across a set of related books, they inevitably notice the similarities and differences in how texts are crafted. Subtle differences across texts that might have escaped a student's notice if he or she approached each book as a singular read—including text structure and features, vocabulary, and presentational formats—come into sharp focus as students concentrate on reading and discussing a set of related texts. (Fountas & Pinnell, 2006)

So it is my view that no book is the exclusive property of a single grade level. We must recognize that every book stands ready and makes the same offering to every reader who comes to the pages. Only those readers who come again and again will ever walk away with the fullness of what is offered. All that to say, yes, one book can become a BFB in more than one grade level. If this is the case, the challenge is for the teacher, not the child— the teacher should know the book and what it has to offer and know the children and what they are ready to take away.

Building Students' Connections to Best Friend Books

It is very likely that your best friends cross your mind when you are away from one another. You may hear a song and be reminded of a trip you took together. You may be shopping and notice something that person would like. You may be reading and run across a phrase your best friend says all the time. You may be pouring a cup of coffee and realize the mug was a birthday gift from that friend. Little things spark your memory and cause you to think of those people who are dear to you. That may prompt you to make a call or send a text or plan an outing. We want to ensure that our students are thinking of BFBs between visits as well.

Here's what I do. Let's assume I've read *Sheila Rae the Brave* by Kevin Henkes. After the first uninterrupted read, I pause for a few seconds and hover in silence with the story. I say something like, "I know this book is about Sheila Rae and she was certainly brave, but I'm still thinking about her little sister, Louise. I'm going to think about Louise for a while before we visit this book again."

Then, after the book is closed and returned to the BFB collection, I will pause at some random moment later that day and at a couple of other times in the next couple of days and say something like, "I'm thinking about *Sheila Rae the Brave* again. She did lots of things to show how brave she was. I need to visit that book again and notice what she thinks it means to be brave." Or, "I was just thinking about Louise. She certainly admires her big sister, Sheila Rae. I remember when I was little, I thought my big brother could do anything. When we visit that book again, I'm going to notice how Louise admires Sheila Rae and learns from her."

The intention here is to model the notion that a story lingers in your thinking well after the last word is read and the cover is closed. I want to prompt the students to think about characters and ideas and issues; I want to plant the notion that readers think about stories and question ideas and generate questions after reading. I want to model this notion and demonstrate how this leads us back to revisit a story with a fresh focus.

Creating a "Buzz" Around Best Friend Books

A Best Friend Book lingers with us after the first visit. It whispers to us and beckons us to return. First impressions are important. Make sure you are thoroughly familiar with the book before you share it with your class. Read it aloud for yourself a few times to find those spots where you need to slow the pace or drop your voice to a whisper. Get to know the characters well enough so that the tone of your voice will convey what they are feeling. Immerse yourself in the story so you will be aware of the subtle (and not so subtle) ways the author builds tension and let your voice signal that as well. Spend time with the illustrations and explore how details in the art open avenues to understanding for the reader.

Then, when you are ready to present the book for the first time, do it with a bit of ceremony. Let your students know this book is one that you hold dear and that you can't wait to share with them. Create a "buzz" around the book. Be clear that this first read is about understanding the story and meeting the characters. Let students know you all will be visiting this book again and again across the year and that you will have several opportunities to look closely at every detail.

Introducing Your BFB Collection to Students

Developing a close friendship takes time. It takes intention and it takes being together. If we want our students to develop this level of understanding and familiarity with a small collection of books, we must have a plan.

Begin as you would if you were introducing two of your friends who don't already know each other. That assumes you believe the two will "hit it off" and find one another interesting. In the first meeting you are the one holding most of the knowledge; you know something about each of the other two people. Likewise, when introducing your students to a BFB for the first time, you will already have insider knowledge of the book and of the children. You'll know that the tension is going to build on the third page. You'll know that the sister is going to get homesick and come home from camp a week early. You'll know that the little brother will act as if this spoils his summer, but he secretly delights in having the sister home again. And you'll also know that in your classroom Nico is missing a sister who went away to college this year. You'll know that Maya is an only child who wishes she had a sister. And you'll know the way the author uses details to build tension is the very thing Anthony is trying to do in his draft. You are the matchmaker in this scenario, so you begin slowly and plan for several future meetings to nurture the friendship you are certain will develop.

The Impact of Best Friend Books on Students' Reading and Writing

We don't expect big changes to occur rapidly. We take our time getting to know each one of the BFBs. We understand that each revisit with a BFB helps us to gain deeper insights about the character or the development of the story, but it also causes us to look at other stories and characters with new insights and fresh questions. Soon we begin to notice students bringing their BFB insights to new titles. We hear it in their comments while conferring. We hear it in their conversations with peers about books. We see it in written responses and notice it in the questions and conversations that emerge from other read-aloud experiences.

Then we carry those ideas forward into our writing work. As readers, we have noticed and wondered and questioned as we revisit our BFBs. We have explored characters and thought about how the writer helped us know them. We have examined their challenges, their motivations, their personalities, their strengths, and their flaws. We have examined the setting and delved into how

HOME VISIT

Connect With Families!
scholastic.com/BFBresources

At school, your students have connected to their Best Friend Books in multiple ways; now invite them to connect their Best Friend Books to their families. Download some simple talking points students can use to guide their BFB conversations at home.

it impacts the characters and the plot. We have thought about the decisions the writer made to set those ideas in motion. We have discovered the places where the tension builds, and we have made note of how the writer made that happen.

We have examined the use of dialogue, the placement of specific details, the choice of a particular concrete noun, and numerous other things in our quest to know this story more intimately. And through all of this we have always looped back to thinking about what the writer (and/or the artist) did to set it up for us.

> "Immature poets imitate, mature poets steal."
>
> —T.S. ELIOT

So now we bring new insights into our writing work. We know how story works and how characters are developed. We understand how to build tension and, more importantly, we know why it needs to happen. We have insights into how pacing works, how transitions take us from one scene to the next and link all the pieces together. We actually think about setting and recognize whether the plot is dependent on certain weather conditions or a particular geography. We understand how dialogue is more than just talk between characters—we know that it can reveal motives and attitudes and emotions, and introduce characters that never make an appearance in the story. We know things about our BFBs that can inform our own decisions as we sit down to plan our next writing project.

Closing Thoughts

Dear friends are with us always. We know that our best friends "have our backs" and will come to our aid in a flash if we need them. In that way, our best friends are always part of us; they are with us even when we can't see them. Our Best Friend Books are like that. They are on reserve, waiting in our minds and hearts. We may even forget they are there until we sit down to read a new book or plan our next writing. Then those BFBs begin to emerge. As we meet new characters, we are reminded of a BFB character. When the plot takes an unexpected twist, we grin and think of how that happened in one of our BFBs. When we begin to read the dialogue between two characters and discover there is a third character we have not yet met, we just chuckle. We know how that works because one of our BFBs did that as well. Yep, those BFBs are there waiting to come to our aid.

CHAPTER 4

Getting to Know a Best Friend Book: The First Visit

"The first reading of a book is a gift we unwrap together. The magic of that moment happens only once."

—LESTER L. LAMINACK

The first read-aloud of a Best Friend Book is a gift. Like any gift, the excitement and joy of unwrapping it to discover the treasure inside is something that can't be relived. Take care with this privilege, do it slowly, and let your students relish the language and the unfolding of the text. There is great satisfaction in the opportunity to come to know a book slowly. Remember, each Best Friend Book will be visited again and again, so there is no need to rush. Don't be in a hurry; you want your Best Friend to make a good first impression.

Starting With the "Movie Read"

I like to call the first read-aloud the "movie read." Imagine that your friend invites you over to watch a movie. Your friend says, "Oh gosh, I love this movie. It's one of my favorites, I know you will love it, too." You agree. When you arrive your friend offers snacks and beverages, reaches for the remote, and turns the TV on. You settle back on the sofa eagerly awaiting the movie. Your friend presses pause and turns toward you. "Now, before I start the movie there are a few things I should explain. The plot is rather complex so I'll explain how it goes before we watch. Also, you need to know there are some unusual special effects in the second scene. Since you don't go to movies as often as I do, you may not get what's going on…." For the next few minutes your friend continues telling you "what you need to know" so you will understand the movie. You smile and nod and hope the movie will start soon. Finally, the movie is running and you are about 15 minutes in. You are engaged with the story line and your friend presses pause. "Hey, this is the part

where those special effects get tricky. Did you notice where…? So, tell me what you think is happening so far. Are you getting it?" You find this disconcerting, even a bit aggravating. But you respond and engage in the conversation. About the time you find yourself getting involved in the ideas of this conversation, your friend says, "OK, let's get back to the movie." And with a press of the play button you find yourself trying to switch from your thoughts about the special effects and the way they impact the plot back to the unfolding story on the screen.

This whole scenario would be absurd to most adults.

When you are going to watch a movie you typically buy your ticket, enter the theater, and watch from start to finish without interruption. There are no commercial breaks. There is no pause button. There is no one on the speaker stopping the movie at critical spots to quiz you, nudge your conversation, interrupt the flow of the story, or clarify anything that might not be clear. That first viewing of a movie is an experience in which you are focused on getting the big picture even though you attend to various details and aspects as the story unfolds. If you are watching with a friend, you may leave the theater in silence as you both reflect, or you may dive into a conversation the second it ends. You and your friend will likely agree on much. However, chances are there will be differences in what you notice and you will likely have a few differences in your interpretations of some aspects of what you saw. The conversation that ensues will likely prompt you to rethink, perhaps even revisit, the movie a second time.

I believe in the power of interactive read-aloud experiences. I have seen powerful insights develop through that experience. However, I firmly believe that every read-aloud experience does not need to be an interactive read-aloud. These Best Friend Books are titles you and your students will visit many times across the year. The first visit, then, is devoted to getting acquainted. The intention of this first visit is to capture interest and attention, to leave the students wanting to talk and ask questions and look back to check on something. In short, the purpose is to entice them to want more. You want them to think, reflect, and talk with each other. You want them to discover the feeling of lingering with a story and thinking about characters after the book is closed. You want them to notice what the writer is doing and how that helps them construct meaning.

SPOTLIGHT ON LESTER VIDEO

Your First Visit With a Best Friend Book: The "Movie Read"

scholastic.com/BFBresources

Our friendships develop in a similar way. When you meet a new person who piques your interest, you are likely to plan another visit or outing together. It would be rare to leave that second meeting knowing everything there is to know about your new friend. But you are likely to leave knowing more, knowing something new. This may lead to more and more time together, and each visit will bring new insights, new questions, and new wonderings as your friendship blossoms over time.

Two things are significant here. First, the friendship (the bonds and depth of caring) does not happen all at once. Rather, it takes time for this to develop. It unfolds slowly and organically, arising from common interests and communication. And secondly, in a friendship there is something that draws you in, something that pulls you toward a second and third and fourth meeting to spend more time together. Perhaps the process of gradually coming to know someone is part of what pulls us to return and spend more time together. Perhaps the process of an emerging friendship is rewarding in itself.

Let's consider this idea with a carefully selected set of books, say five books for each grade level. Think about a set of books you know very well, books you have turned to over and over again across the year. Think of a single title you bring into your classroom community every year. Think of that title as a best friend who has been with you for several years. So this year you are going to introduce this title as you would introduce a best friend.

The first visit is an opportunity to get acquainted, so I say something like this:

I have a book I can't wait to share with you. I have loved this book for a long time and I think you will love it, too. [Hold the book facing the students.] *It is called* [say the title] *and it is written by* [say the author's name] *and the illustrator is* [say the illustrator's name]. *This is one of my Best Friend Books and we are going to visit with this book several times this year. Soon each of us will know this book like we know our own best friends. So, for this first visit we can take our time and enjoy every word. Today, I'll read from the first page to the last without stopping, just like going to a movie.* [Read the book.]

> *"From my own experience I realize that the literature I heard, rather than read, as a child resonates again and again in my memory whenever I sit down to write."*
>
> —**MEM FOX**

Of course, each BFB will have a personality of its own. The tone and mood will be a bit different for each title. The characters will be developed in a variety of ways. Voice will vary from book to book. Read each book carefully before you share it with your class. Read it aloud a few times, and find the rhythm and shifts in intensity that set the mood of the book. Let your voice reflect the tone of the narrator and the personality of each character. Note the shifts in emotion, and echo those in your voice as you read. This first read-aloud is important. It is the introduction to a new best friend.

Examples of First Visits With Best Friend Books

On the following pages, you can find examples for how you can introduce students to Best Friend Books for the first time. Remember that the goal is to not interrupt the experience of the book during this first "movie read" but to know that you'll be revisiting the book again and again in the coming days, weeks, or months and will have plenty of time for further study and inquiry.

FIRST VISIT WITH BEST FRIEND BOOK (KINDERGARTEN)

Owen, written and illustrated by Kevin Henkes

CHARACTERS

- **Owen**—young boy (mouse) who is about to enter school (main character)
- **Mom**—caring and supportive
- **Dad**—caring and supportive
- **Mrs. Tweezers**—adult neighbor who offers advice to Owen's parents (catalyst for tension)

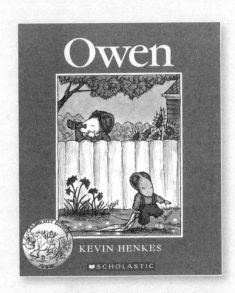

SETTING

Owen's home and yard

PLOT

Owen has a favorite blanket (Fuzzy) that he takes EVERYWHERE. Owen will start school soon. Fuzzy is getting worn and his neighbor, Mrs. Tweezers, suggests several times that Owen is just too big for the blanket. Mrs. Tweezers makes several suggestions for getting Owen to give it up. Though his parents try them all, none of them work. Finally, Owen's mom arrives at a solution to make a collection of handkerchiefs from Fuzzy.

PERSPECTIVE

Text is presented from the main character's perspective.

POINT OF VIEW

Third person

1 Remember this "movie read" is your first meeting with a new best friend. Just read and relish knowing you will return for a closer look and much talk. Here are a few things to keep in mind during your first read:

- Owen is a very happy child who loves his blanket.

- His parents seem totally unconcerned about his attachment to his blanket until Mrs. Tweezers starts to offer her suggestions.

- Mrs. Tweezers seems to be a bit of a busybody. She has grown children and believes it is her obligation to make sure others benefit from her experience and "wisdom."

- Notice how the tone shifts slightly when Owen's parents become concerned about Fuzzy.

- Owen's parents try Mrs. Tweezers' suggestions but remain supportive of Owen. He is never pushed or forced to give up Fuzzy.

2 After reading, encourage reflection by asking students one of the following questions:

- *Which character are you thinking about right now?*

- *What are you wondering?*

- *What surprised you in this story?*

3 Over the next few days, prior to your return visit, bring up the book from time to time. You want to keep the characters and the story fresh in students' minds.

Your intention here is to model the notion that experiences with stories linger after we leave the book. You want to nudge students' thinking and spark conversation about the book between visits. Perhaps you say something like:

- *You know, when we were reading* Owen, *I kept thinking that Fuzzy was almost like Owen's very best friend.*

- *I keep thinking about Mrs. Tweezers. I'm not sure why she kept telling Owen's mom and dad to take Fuzzy away. We may need to think about that when we visit with her again.*

- *I was just thinking about Owen. I remember how the words told us how much he loves Fuzzy. As I think about that, I remember seeing things in the art. Maybe we should visit* Owen *again and look closely at those illustrations.*

FIRST VISIT WITH BEST FRIEND BOOK (GRADE 3)

Jamaica's Find, written by Juanita Havill and illustrated by Anne Sibley O'Brien

CHARACTERS

- **Jamaica**—six-year-old girl (main character)
- **Mother**—Jamaica's mom (kind, supportive, encouraging)
- **Father**—appears in only one scene
- **Brother**—appears in only one scene
- **Young Man**—works in the park office
- **Kristin**—young girl at the park, playmate

SETTING

The park and Jamaica's home

PLOT

Jamaica finds a hat and a stuffed dog at the park. She decides to keep the dog. When she arrives home, it comes to her attention that another little girl may be missing that dog. Jamaica is flooded with emotions and decides to return the dog to the young man behind the counter at the park house. The next morning at the park, Jamaica meets a new friend, Kristin, and discovers that she lost her favorite Edgar dog at the park the day before. The two girls race to the park house to reunite Kristin and Edgar dog.

PERSPECTIVE

Text is presented from the main character's perspective.

POINT OF VIEW

Third person

SPOTLIGHT ON LESTER VIDEO

A First Visit With *Jamaica's Find* by Juanita Havill

scholastic.com/BFBresources

1 I want you to meet one of my Best Friend Books. This one is called *Jamaica's Find*. It is written by Juanita Havill and illustrated by Anne Sibley O'Brien. Since this is our first visit with *Jamaica's Find*, I'll read it from start to finish without stopping. I'll read through and at the end we'll take a few minutes to think about it before we move on to our work for the day.

- Note the tone of our narrator remains supportive, matter-of-fact, and even.
- Read it at a moderate pace, letting your voice signal where there is some inner conflict for Jamaica.
- Distinguish between the voice of our narrator and the characters. Mother's voice is calm, supportive, and encouraging. Father and Brother speak only once each, but their voices are distinctive. Let your voice capture Brother's mocking tone and Father's matter-of-fact directness. Note how Jamaica's voice will shift with her mood as she struggles with the inner conflict of what to do with the dog.
- The narrator's voice is steady and calm.

2 As you conclude the book, offer a comment to prompt thinking. This is not the time for extended conversation. Remember this is the "get acquainted" visit only. Get interest flowing and remind students to keep thinking about the story. Be sure to let them know that you will be revisiting this book soon. Sample first-read questions:

- What did you think of the story?
- What does this make you wonder?
- What surprised you?
- What did you notice?
- Which character are you thinking about right now?

3 Bring closure to the conversation and leave students with a comment that will invite continued thinking about the story. Here are a few suggestions:

- Jamaica thought it was OK to keep the dog. Then she changed her mind. Think about what led her to make that decision.
- Mother never told Jamaica that she had to take the dog back to the park. Think about how Mother helped Jamaica decide for herself.
- Jamaica found two things at the park, a hat and the stuffed dog. She decided to turn one in to lost and found. She decided to keep the other. Let's think about why she did that.

4 Over the next few days, prior to your return visit, bring up the book from time to time. You want to keep the characters and the story fresh in students' minds. You might say something like:

- I keep thinking about Jamaica finding that little dog in the park. I could tell she really liked it. We should revisit that page and look closely at the art as we read those words.
- I'm thinking about *Jamaica's Find* again. I remember Jamaica sitting on her bed when she heard the pots rattle and then heard her mother's steps coming down the hall. I'm wondering what she was thinking. When we revisit the story, let's examine every scene and consider what Jamaica is thinking throughout the story.
- I've been thinking about Kristin in *Jamaica's Find*. Her face looked so sad. She must have been missing Edgar dog so much. When we revisit, let's think about her the whole time.

FIRST VISIT FOR BEST FRIEND BOOK (GRADE 5)

Crow Call, written by Lois Lowry and illustrated by Bagram Ibatoulline

CHARACTERS

- **Lizzie**—younger of two sisters (main character)

- **Jessica**—older sister, offers a point of contrast giving us a bit of insight into Lizzie's personality

- **Daddy**—has been away fighting in a war and feels like a stranger to Lizzie

- **Salesman and a waitress**— these secondary characters provide situations that allow us to witness Lizzie and Daddy react and interact

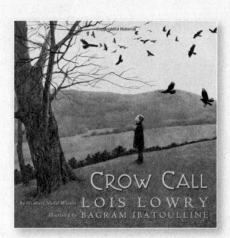

SETTING

Rural farming community in Pennsylvania, November 1945

PLOT

Father has been away for a long time and has returned from service in the war. Lizzie is getting reacquainted with her father and is groping toward getting to know him, to even be comfortable saying "Daddy" out loud. A hunting trip to reduce the crow population on the farm becomes the vehicle for forging trust, understanding, and communication.

PERSPECTIVE

Text is presented from the main character's perspective.

POINT OF VIEW

First person

1 Since this is our first visit with *Crow Call*, I'll read it aloud from start to finish without stopping. Just listen and think, but hold your comments and questions until later. After I finish, we'll take a few moments to sit with this story and think about it before we move on to our work for the day.

- Note this text is a memoir story set in the mid-1940s when the narrator reunites with her father who was been away in the war for a long time. There is a bit of awkward searching to reconnect and find a place of comfort with her father who has just returned.

- The narrator is a young girl (eight or nine years old). She is speaking in the present tense. Let your voice reflect her innocence and concern. This is not the exuberance of going to a birthday party. Take your time and let the budding relationship unfold as it would in real time.

- The story illustrates features from the era that surface in the art—the visit to the store where the shirt is purchased, and the breakfast at the diner. However, the heart of this story is the process of rebuilding a parent-child relationship that was interrupted by external circumstances. Let your voice convey Lizzie's initial hesitancy and uncertainty, and then her becoming more confident and comfortable with her father's presence in her life.

- Note that the father's patience, his calm and supportive manner, reveals his insights. Let your voice reflect his supportive tone.

2 As you conclude the book, close it and sit in silence for a few seconds. Remind your students that this story represents a true moment in time. Then read the author's note on the last page. Remember that this is the "get acquainted" visit only. You want your students to be eager to reflect and think and talk. Be sure to let them know you will be visiting this book again very soon. This book has depth and substance that provide opportunities for varied points of entry into conversation and discussion. Pose one question and invite your students to write for two minutes.

Sample questions:

- *What surprised you about this story?*

- *What would you like to go back to and explore in this story?*

- *What did you think about while listening to this story?*

- *What does this story make you wonder?*

- *Which character are you thinking about right now? What are you thinking?*

3 Over the next few days, prior to your return visit, bring up the book from time to time. You want to keep the characters and the story fresh in students' minds. You might say something like:

- *I keep thinking about Lizzie. She seems to be younger than you, maybe eight or nine, so maybe in third or fourth grade. If her father had been away in the war for a long time, I am wondering how old she was when he left. I wonder how much she remembers about him.*

- *I'm remembering the scene where Lizzie and her dad were sitting at the counter in the diner. That waitress seemed shocked when Lizzie's father ordered three pieces of pie. When we visit* Crow Call *again, let's think about all the things the father did and why.*

- *I was just thinking about the first page of* Crow Call. *I love the language on that page. Now that we have read the whole story, we will slow down and think about that page on our next visit. I think it will mean much more this time.*

- *I'm thinking of* Crow Call *again. Remember that scene where Lizzie is in the car sitting next to her father? I remember the two of them looking right out the window. I could almost feel how uncomfortable she was. When we visit* Crow Call *next, let's pause on that page and look closely at what Lizzie was thinking and feeling.*

Closing Thoughts

First impressions are important. Take the time to be prepared and know each Best Friend Book intimately before you make the introduction to your students. Trust the author and the illustrator of each book to know their audience; resist the urge to frontload meaning. Trust your teaching. You've led mini-lessons with the whole class, shared reading and guided reading lessons with small groups, and conferred with individuals. Trust your work. And finally, trust your students to enjoy the story and make meaning for themselves in this first meeting. Remember that you'll be visiting these Best Friend Books again and again. In those visits, you will have many opportunities to focus on individual elements and amplify what you feel is important. Give yourself permission to slow down and build a solid relationship between your students and each title. Remember that deep and lasting friendships are formed over time.

CHAPTER 5

Building Relationships: Return Visits With a Best Friend Book

"The more we read, the more we know—and, therefore, the more expansive our capacity to comprehend."

—WALTER KINTSCH, PROFESSOR EMERITUS OF PSYCHOLOGY AND NEUROSCIENCE

After the first visit (the movie read), you will plan several more visits. As with any developing friendship, take it slowly and enjoy each visit. Remember, there is no need to feel you must share every insight you have about the book, or lift out every teaching point you've unearthed, or highlight all the opportunities for inferring, or note each of the cause-and-effect links in the first and second visits.

The joy here is taking the time to discover, to delve in, and to savor the moments when students see the power of literature. Slow down and be open to the world of possibilities that will emerge. It has been my experience that each focused visit with a BFB becomes a scaffold for the next visit. The layering of insight upon insight is powerful because it comes in "bite-sized" bits that students chew on and take with them into their book clubs and independent reading and later bring to the surface in their own writing.

WHAT THE RESEARCH SAYS

Proficient reading—which entails high-level comprehension—is a complex process, involving an intricate orchestration of multiple skills, strategies, and conceptual understandings also known as *systems of strategic actions*. (Fountas & Pinnell, 2006) "Text comprehension requires the involvement of many different components, relying upon many different kinds of information and yielding complex mental representations.... However, text comprehension is not simply the sum of the activity of these various processes, but arises from their *coordinated* operation as a system." (Kintsch & Rawson, 2005) Each reader builds a system for processing texts that begins with early reading behaviors and becomes a network of strategic activities for reading increasingly complex texts. (Fountas & Pinnell, 2006)

Let's think about what happens when we revisit a BFB again and again. Take a moment and turn your left hand over. Now look at your palm. You are looking at a story map. Consider this:

I like to tell students we can hold our new BFB in our hand. Then I summarize the story with these five fingers:

FINGER	TEACHER TALK	KID TALK
Thumb	Initiating event	How did it get started?
Index finger	Rising action	It's getting interesting!
Middle finger	Problem/tension/climax	Now we know the problem.
Ring finger	Solving problem/falling action	How did they try to solve it?
Pinky	Conclusion	What finally happened?

Holding the story in your hand gives us some common ground to think about the story over time. I may say something like, "I was thinking about *Peter's Chair* again." I hold up my hand and look at it.

- I put my thumb up: "Peter was building towers with his blocks when Willie ran through and knocked them down."

- I lift my index finger: "Mom reminded him to play quietly because there is a new baby in the house. Peter peeked in and saw his dad painting his old crib."

- I lift my middle finger: "Peter's feeling sad and maybe jealous."

- I lift my ring finger: "Peter takes his chair and a few things and runs away to the sidewalk with Willie."

- I lift my pinky: "Peter realizes he is too big for baby furniture and helps his dad paint the chair for Susie."

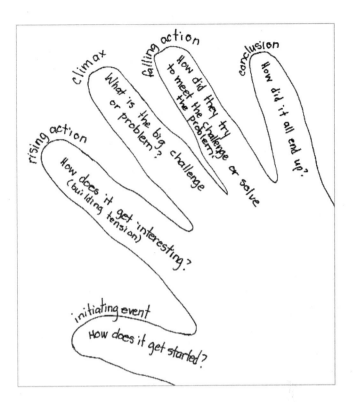

I may revisit that a few times to help set the essence of the story in their minds. Over the course of the day I may make the following observations:

- "I keep thinking about Peter. I believe he felt pretty sad for a little while. I want to revisit *Peter's Chair* and look closely at his face. Maybe that will help me know what he was feeling."

- "I've been thinking about Peter's mother. I can't be sure if she noticed that he was feeling sad and a little jealous. Help me remember to look for that when we visit with *Peter's Chair* again."

- "You know, I've been thinking about Peter. I think he is the kind of boy who gets upset, but he can change his mind. Let's think about what we know about Peter and try to decide."

The intention is to model that books, stories, and characters linger in your thinking and prompt new questions and insights that lead you back to the page. Each of these "random thoughts" will be a lens for our focus in a future visit.

It is my experience that we don't take in all the nuances of a character, the elements of story, or the techniques employed by the writer in a single visit. I find it necessary to revisit as insights develop and new questions take shape. Likewise, we will have several visits with a BFB and each of them will have a specific purpose. As I plan the return visits, I explore the story with these ideas in mind:

HOME VISIT

Take the Story Map Home
scholastic.com/BFBresources

Download a story map for your students to share with their families—a simplified version that they can use with a well-known folktale from their own communities or with a well-known fairy tale such as *Goldilocks and the Three Bears*.

CHARACTERS

- How many characters are in the story? Which character is the main character?

- How do the other characters help me get to know the main character?

- What is the purpose of each character in the story? How does each character contribute to the story?

- Does the main character change across the story? If so, how?

- How does the main character work to meet the challenge or solve the problem?

- How do the other characters contribute to the challenge? Solution?

SETTING

- Where is this happening? What is the physical location?

- Is it a real place? (playground, apartment) Or is it imagined in the character's mind? (an old box becomes a fort)

- What is the weather? Climate? Season? And how does this impact the characters and their decisions?

- Does the setting make a difference or is it just a backdrop for events?

PLOT

- How does the story get started?

- Where and how is tension built?

WHAT THE RESEARCH SAYS

Frank Serafini, who is a literacy researcher as well as a picture book author and photographer, offers unique insights into the role illustrations and graphics play in today's sophisticated picture books. He writes:

"The illustrations and visual elements contained in picture books may well be the first time young children are exposed to art and artistic techniques. Young readers are drawn into the world of reading and literature through the images and artwork contained in picture books. As readers get older, the picture books that are intended for them become more sophisticated. The media used to create the illustrations, the interplay between visual elements and written text, and the meanings and significance of the visual elements in picture books become more complex. Contemporary picture book illustrators draw upon a wide variety of artistic techniques including realism, surrealism, impressionism, cubism, and postmodernism to create their illustrations and visual elements. Making connections between the art in picture books and classic art forms and styles can increase older reader appreciation of art itself. The art contained in picture books may be a door into the world of art that older readers need to make connections to the vast array of visual elements in other texts and experience." (Serafini, 2008)

- What are the challenges or problems for the character(s)?
- What is attempted in an effort to meet the challenge or solve the problem?
- How does the plot move forward?
- How is the plot organized? What structures are employed? What impact do they have?

ART

- How do the illustrations work to reveal mood and tone?
- Do the illustrations hold a key to information not presented in the text?
- Do the illustrations parallel, support, extend, or enrich the text?
- Are there questions raised by the text that can be answered by a close examination of the art?
- What do we learn about the setting by a close examination of the art?
- What do we learn about the character(s) by a close examination of the art?

INTERPLAY (How all these factors work together to build a story)

- How are the challenges/problems linked to place, weather, or to the personality of the character?
- How do the physical location and weather conditions impact the characters?
- How do the character's fears, worries, dreams, and favorites impact the plot?
- Technique: (author and/or illustrator decisions)
- Examine what the author and/or illustrator has done to lead us toward these insights.

Examples of Return Visits With Best Friend Books

Here are some examples (using the same three picture books we mentioned in the previous chapter) for topics you can focus on when you revisit your Best Friend Books with students.

HOME VISIT

Take Home *Owen*, *Jamaica's Find*, and *Crow Call*

scholastic.com/BFBresources

Invite your students to introduce their families to the Best Friend Books *Owen*, *Jamaica's Find*, and *Crow Call*. Download simple story guides that they can share with their families to support the conversation.

SPOTLIGHT ON LESTER VIDEO

Return Visits With *Owen* and *Crow Call*

scholastic.com/BFBresources

RETURN VISITS WITH A BEST FRIEND BOOK (KINDERGARTEN)

Owen, written and illustrated by Kevin Henkes

TOPICS TO DISCUSS	EVIDENCE IN THE BOOK
Identifying Qualities of the Main Character Every story has a main character and Owen is the main character in this one. We know that he loves Fuzzy, his blanket. Let's visit again and think about other things we know about Owen.	• Owen likes to play outside. • Owen sucks his thumb. • Owen believes Fuzzy likes the same things he likes. • Owen is playful (we see him in several scenes playing with Fuzzy). • Owen gets worried sometimes (blanket fairy). • Owen is clever and can solve problems (blanket fairy, vinegar trick). • Owen uses his imagination (Captain Plunger, becoming invisible).
Identifying the Main Character's Problem The main character in a story has a problem to solve or a challenge to face. We have decided that Owen's challenge is finding a way to keep Fuzzy even though the grown-ups think he is too big for a blanket. Let's visit again and notice all the ways Owen tries to keep Fuzzy.	• Owen loves Fuzzy and wants to keep him. • We see Mrs. Tweezers talking with Owen's parents several times. She tells them he is too old to play with Fuzzy. • Owen's parents try the blanket fairy, the vinegar trick, and saying "no." • Owen doesn't want to give up Fuzzy.
Identifying Other Characters in a Story In addition to a main character, writers may also include other characters to help us think about important ideas. In this story, Kevin Henkes includes a neighbor named Mrs. Tweezers. In this visit, let's focus our thinking on Mrs. Tweezers. Let's think about why she is important in this story. Remember we may need to examine the illustrations and think about the language.	• Mrs. Tweezers is peeking around the fence on the first page. She is watching Owen hold Fuzzy and suck his thumb. • On the second spread we see Mrs. Tweezers leaning over the fence whispering to Owen's parents. She is telling them he is too old to play with Fuzzy. She tells them about the blanket fairy. • On the sixth spread we see Mrs. Tweezers standing on flower pots by the fence and talking with Owen's parents. She is telling them Owen can't be a baby forever and tells them about the vinegar trick.

TOPICS TO DISCUSS	EVIDENCE IN THE BOOK
Identifying Other Characters in a Story continued	• On the ninth spread we see Mrs. Tweezers think about the language. She tells Owen's parents he can't take that blanket to school and she tells them to say "no." • On the last page we see Mrs. Tweezers at the fence. She and Owen wave to each other with their handkerchiefs. NOTE: Mrs. Tweezers helps to create tension, she helps us discover the problem and gives Owen and his parents something to overcome or solve.
Identifying Feelings by Looking at the Art **Fuzzy was very important to Owen. Let's visit this time and think about Fuzzy. Let's think about why Fuzzy is so important to Owen. We may need to look closely at the art and look at Owen's face to find out.**	• First page: We see Owen cuddled with Fuzzy. His eyes are closed and he is sucking his thumb. He looks content. • First spread: We see Owen in six small illustrations and one larger one. In each illustration, Owen is doing something with Fuzzy. They are never apart. • Second spread: We see Owen using Fuzzy to pull a little toy bird behind him. We also see Owen getting ready for bed and he is holding Fuzzy. He looks concerned about the blanket fairy. • Third spread: Owen stuffs Fuzzy into his pajama pants so the blanket fairy can't take Fuzzy. He looks happy and relieved. • Fourth spread: Owen hides Fuzzy behind his back when his parents are talking about Fuzzy being dirty and ratty. He looks worried. Owen wears Fuzzy as a cape when he is Captain Plunger and puts Fuzzy over his head when he is invisible. He looks happy. • Fifth spread: Owen clutches Fuzzy when he has his nails trimmed, gets a haircut, and visits the dentist. His face shows concern or worry. • Sixth spread: Owen rubs Fuzzy in the sandbox and buries it in the garden to get the vinegar smell out. Owen looks playful and delighted. • Seventh spread: Owen uses Fuzzy as a flag to wrap himself in and as a wagon to pull his toys behind him. He takes a bath with Fuzzy and sleeps with it and twists it tightly while watching TV. He looks happy and content in all but one illustration. • Eighth spread: Owen holds on to Fuzzy even when he is playing in a yard filled with toys and hides his face with Fuzzy when he is crying. • Ninth spread: Owen clings to Fuzzy while his parents try to comfort him. He watches with a bit of trepidation while his mother snips and sews Fuzzy. Owen looks worried. He has tears in his eyes. • Tenth spread: Owen now has a collection of small Fuzzies, and he takes one everywhere. He looks happy.

RETURN VISITS WITH A BEST FRIEND BOOK (GRADE 3)

Jamaica's Find, written by Juanita Havill and illustrated by Anne Sibley O'Brien

TOPICS TO DISCUSS	EVIDENCE IN THE BOOK
Identifying How Characters Are Revealed **Characters are revealed through:** • **third person narrator** • **dialogue** • **actions**	The narrator tells us what Jamaica does. • Stops at the park to play • Finds a hat and a dog • Takes the dog home Jamaica's dialogue is a window into her thinking and decisions. • "It [hat] didn't fit me." • "I like the dog." • "Do I have to, Mother? I don't feel good," • "Mother, I want to take the dog back to the park," Jamaica's actions reveal her thoughts and character. • She put the dog in her basket. • She took the dog to her room. • She looked at the dog and tossed it on the chair. • She took the dog back to the park and turned it in at the Lost and Found.
Identifying Important Details in a Story	In the scene where Jamaica finds the hat and the dog, we are given two details about the hat (red, sock hat) and eight details about the dog (stuffed, cuddly, gray, worn, stains, button nose missing, white spot, two black ears). The use of details signals the importance of the dog in the plot.

TOPICS TO DISCUSS	EVIDENCE IN THE BOOK
Identifying the Importance of Setting Setting is integral to the plot and includes: • **emotional climate** • **physical space**	The park is a community space where many children play. Things get lost and found there. Jamaica's home is a closed space where her family's support helps focus her thinking.
Identifying the Feelings of Other Characters Mother is supportive and provides a scaffold that allows us to discover Jamaica's character.	• "Maybe the dog doesn't fit you either." • "It probably belongs to a girl just like Jamaica." • "Mother came in quietly, sat down by Jamaica ... didn't say anything ... put her arms around Jamaica...." • "We'll go first thing in the morning."
Identifying How Details Help Readers Understand a Character	• "Jamaica heard the pots rattle. Then she heard her mother's steps." • "'Yes,' said Jamaica, feeling hot around her ears." • "I'm sure some little girl or boy will come in after it today, a nice little dog like that...." • "Yes, but I have to find something first ... Edgar dog. I brought him with me yesterday and now I can't find him...."

RETURN VISITS WITH A BEST FRIEND BOOK (GRADE 5)

Crow Call, written by Lois Lowry and illustrated by Bagram Ibatoulline

TOPICS TO DISCUSS	EVIDENCE IN THE BOOK
Identifying Traits of the Main Character The narrator in *Crow Call* is Lizzie, the main character. **Notice the ways we find out about Lizzie:** • narration • dialogue • interior monologue/ thinking • actions • reactions	Lizzie is a little timid with her dad. • She feels her father is a stranger because he has been gone away in the war so long. • Saying *"Daddy"* feels new, maybe awkward because she has to whisper it under her breath a few times. • She is concerned about not knowing what to do when they go hunting She wants to do things with her dad, to make him proud of her, to be like him in some ways. • She wants (and gets) a plaid hunting shirt like her dad's even though it is a man's shirt and it is much too big. • She sits with him at the counter in the diner, her pigtails are tucked inside the collar of the big shirt and the waitress mistakes her for a boy. Father winks at her and she wishes the pigtails would stay hidden. Lizzie is thoughtful, kind, and empathetic. • "I wish the crows didn't eat the crops." • "They might have babies to take care of. Baby crows." • "'Look, Daddy,' I whisper. 'Do you see them? They think I'm a crow?' … 'Listen, Daddy! Do you hear them? They think I'm their friend! Maybe their baby, all grown up!'"
Identifying Actions of Other Characters Lizzie and her father are spending a day together and getting to know each other again. On this visit with *Crow Call*, let's look closely at the father and notice what he does to help Lizzie get to know and trust him after his long absence.	• He buys her the hunting shirt she wanted even though her sister insists it is a man's shirt and the salesman hesitates. He said, "You know, Lizzie … buying this shirt is probably a very practical thing to do. You will never outgrow this shirt." • In the diner, when the waitress mistakes Lizzie for a boy, Daddy winks at Lizzie and they play along. It's as if the two of them have a secret joke. • He orders three pieces of cherry pie, one for himself and two for Lizzie. • When Lizzie shares her concern for the baby crows that may be left behind, we gain insight into her fears of what would happen if her daddy had gotten shot in the war. Father explains there would be no crow babies at this time of year. • When Lizzie begins sounding the crow call, her father watches her delight and listens as she speculates that the crows believe she is one of their friends, or maybe even one of their babies all grown up.

TOPICS TO DISCUSS	EVIDENCE IN THE BOOK

Identifying Autobiographical Details

Let's read the author's note and see what we can glean. Then let's revisit the story with that in mind.

The author's note on the last page shows Lois Lowry at the age of eight wearing the plaid flannel shirt in this story. We learn these events happened in her life in 1945. The note also reminds us of the more central message that parents and children work to build relationships and trust, and grow toward understanding one another.

Identifying Rich Language

Writers use rich language, precise nouns, and strong verbs to help us construct our understanding of the story. In this visit, let's zoom in on those places where Lois Lowry's choice of words helps us know what it was like to be in this place on that day.

Setting [time or season]

- "It's morning, early, barely light, cold for November. …"
- "… the gray-green hills of early morning."
- "Grass, frozen after its summer softness, crunches under our feet. …"
- "… kicking the dead leaves …"
- "It is quieter than summer."

Setting [place or location]

- "across the Pennsylvania farmlands."
- "'Not now, Liz, not this time of year,' he says. 'By now their babies are grown …'"

Setting [weather or climate]

- "Grass, frozen after its summer softness, crunches under our feet; the air is sharp and supremely clear, free from the floating pollens of summer, and our words seem etched and breakable on the brittle stillness."
- "Our breath is steam."

Identifying Important Story Elements

The crow call and the plaid hunting shirt are very important items in this story. As we visit today, let's slow down and look closely in those places where the shirt and the crow call are featured. Let's think about why these two items are so very important in this story.

- Second spread: Note the shirt is in the scene and is described almost like a robe.
- Fourth spread: Note this scene is a flashback to explain the story of the shirt and gives it greater significance.
- Fifth and sixth spreads: Here in the diner scene, the shirt hides Lizzie's pigtails and the waitress mistakes her for a boy. This becomes an inside joke between Lizzie and her father.
- Eleventh spread: In this scene, the father tells Lizzie to sound the crow call. Lizzie's comments (as narrator) give us insight into the importance she assigns to this job.
- Twelfth spread: Now many crows have gathered. The tree limbs are filled with crows like ripe fruit. Lizzie has moved away from her father and stands near the top of the hill. Her delight in this is obvious.

Closing Thoughts

Young children request the same book over and over. Ask any parent or grandparent caring for a toddler or a preschooler. Yet, at school, it seems we are in such a rush to get things done that we attempt to unpack all we can pull from a book in one reading. The power of visiting and having several return visits with a book is that it builds on what young children have already shown us. They need time to relish the familiar as they build a context that enables them to examine and notice the nuances that may often be overlooked in our rush to cover.

CHAPTER 6

The Art of the Read-Aloud

"Use beautiful, content-rich, age- and grade-appropriate picture books—short stories or poetry or short informational pieces illustrated with beautiful art—as a foundation for thinking, talking, and writing."

—IRENE FOUNTAS AND GAY SU PINNELL

For just a few moments, try to conjure up an image in your mind of a parent holding a toddler and telling a story. Perhaps the story is "Goldilocks and the Three Bears" or "The Gingerbread Man" or "Little Red Riding Hood." It might even be a simple nursery rhyme such as "Little Miss Muffet." Now that you have the image, lean in and listen to the telling of the story. Listen to the voice of the storyteller and notice the differences in the pitch when Papa Bear speaks and when Mama Bear speaks. Notice how the pacing changes as the tension in the story begins to mount. Listen to the storyteller stretch out words like "great big papa bear bowl" and increase the speed to push words together when the action is fast-paced. Notice as you listen to the shift in the voice when a character is frightened or angry or excited. When we tell stories, it seems almost natural for us to unconsciously attend to the significant role that tone, intensity, pacing, and mood can play in helping the child make sense of the story. It seems natural as a scaffold for comprehension when we are telling our little ones a story. Before you let go of that image, take a look at the face of the storyteller. You probably notice facial expressions and body language and hand gestures that attempt to make the language easier to understand. Each aspect of the storyteller's rendition of the story is a layer to help the child make meaning, to engage the child in the story, and to create a bond between the humans involved.

Indulge me further and conjure a second image. This time, picture an adult reading a book aloud to a small group of children. The group may be siblings, cousins, or friends gathered for a party, a sleepover, or a playdate. The group may be a group of schoolchildren. Let's say the book is a picture book. Now lean in and listen. Do you hear those shifts in pitch to signal a different character is speaking? Do you hear the elongations of selected words being stretched for emphasis? Do you hear the pacing change when the action is mounting? Do you see the reader using facial expressions or hand gestures that match the story? For some reason, these things seem less natural to adults in a read-aloud than in storytelling.

Reading aloud well borrows from the art of storytelling. To present the text with an accurate rendition of the words but without attention to tone, intensity, mood, and pacing is like leaving the icing off the cake. To read aloud without attention to rhythm, pitch, and stress makes the sound of the reading expressionless, less robust, less meaningful, just… less. Whether it's a first visit or a return visit, to read aloud well, the reader, like the storyteller, must attend to at least these four qualities.

HOME VISIT

Introduce Families to the Joy of the Read-Aloud
scholastic.com/BFBresources

Invite families to watch Lester in action as he demonstrates the most engaging ways to share a Best Friend Book. Check the online Home Visit section for videos that can be used with families along with a URL you can provide for easy access. You can also share these videos at a Family Literacy Event or Back-to-School Night.

1. TONE. I think of the tone of the text as the attitude of the text. Is it chatty and informal, sincere, snarky, caustic, arrogant, formal and distant, cheerful, solemn, or academic? The writer's attitude and feeling toward the subject will set the tone. Tone may also reflect what the writer intends to make the reader feel. In the read-aloud your voice should reflect the tone of the text.

2. MOOD. I think of the mood of a text as the emotional climate of the piece, its temperament, or the way it leaves the reader feeling. Is it sad, depressed, hopeful, wishful, excited, eager, or nostalgic? Often the setting, voice, and personality of the character will help establish mood. As we reach the end of the reading, the mood should linger like a fragrance.

3. INTENSITY. I think of intensity as the energy of the text. Is it powerful and bold, or tender and quiet? Does the energy build and wane? Or does it launch with a punch and remain at that level? Or does it begin full and slowly dwindle? Perhaps it is quiet and gentle from the first line to the last. The intensity of a piece will be reflected in a read-aloud by the shifts in volume and the power of the reader's voice.

4. PACING. I think of pacing as the heartbeat of the text. It is a pulse, a rhythm that creates the flow of the language. It may race at times and slow to heart-stopping standstill at others. We feel the effect of pacing when the reader's voice employs a dramatic pause or begins rushing to build tension. We feel the effect when a reader's voice moves as slow as honey on a February morning to draw the listener in. It may be heard and felt when a reader stretches a word for emphasis or runs through words like a babbling brook to reflect the action of the piece.

Reading aloud well is like playing music. As the reader, you are a musician of sorts and your instrument is your voice. Not only must you (the reader) be able to "read" the words with accuracy, you must also be able to interpret the intentions of the writer regarding tone, intensity, pacing, and mood. The texts we read aloud for our students have signals that indicate the intentions of writers (and the team of people who work in layout and design to produce a book), which are in many ways like the signals provided by composers for musicians.

"There's no exact right way of reading aloud, other than to try to be as expressive as possible. As we read a story, we need to be aware of our body posture, our eyes and their expression, our eye contact with the child or children, our vocal variety, and our general facial animation. But each of us will have our own special way of doing it."

—**MEM FOX**

SPOTLIGHT ON LESTER VIDEO

More on the Art of the Read-Aloud

scholastic.com/BFBresources

For example, in music, when a composer intends for the musician to increase or decrease the intensity of the music, this may be signaled by special marks, which look something like an elongated greater-than sign (<) for an increase or *crescendo*, or an elongated less-than sign (>) for a decrease or *decrescendo*. The musician interprets these notations and adjusts the sound or level of intensity when playing. These shifts in intensity not only capture the attention of the listeners, but they also help convey the emotional content of the music.

Composers also indicate their intentions regarding the pacing of a piece with a time signature (3/4, 4/4, etc.) indicating the number of beats in each measure. This sets a pace, or creates a rhythm for the piece. So a series of whole notes, where each measure is a single note being played for four beats, may seem slow and languid to the ear. However, the composer may create a sense of movement by placing two half-notes, getting two beats each in one measure, followed by a measure with four quarter-notes, getting one beat each. And to create a greater sense of urgency, we may find a measure with eighth notes and sixteenth notes. If the composer decides that a span of silence would create a desired effect, that will be signaled by a rest. The use of silence is an important part of music. Silence in well-chosen places draws your attention to the music. The composer can create a feeling or tone with the combination of pacing and intensity.

Readers can find signals regarding intensity and pacing in print as well. Just as composers use visual cues to signal their intentions, writers use punctuation and shifts in font, bold print, underlining and italics, size of print, syllable length, word length and sentence length, line breaks, white space, and more to indicate their intentions regarding intensity in the performance of the text. As a reader, you recognize that a word printed in bold type suggests that you should increase the intensity of your voice. Likewise, when the print becomes gradually smaller, you would let your voice become gradually softer. Intensity may also be signaled with punctuation marks. Every first-grade student clearly understands that an exclamation point signals excitement. Even first graders know that means your voice becomes stronger and louder. If the writer includes more than one exclamation point, all capital letters, bold print, red lettering, and a larger font, you recognize immediately that you are expected to boost the volume and convey some big message. And if you just read right past that, children will stop you in midsentence and point to the writer's signals, letting you know you didn't read that right. As readers, we come to recognize that a question mark at the end of a line signals a shift in intensity and tone. Ellipses indicate that we should let our voices trail off as if there was more to say but it was better left unsaid, or to indicate that there was a word left out deliberately. It is our voices that communicate these purposes to the listener.

> *"The ups and downs of our voices and our pauses and points of emphasis are like music, literally, to the ears of young children, and kids love music."*
>
> **— MEM FOX**

INSIDE THE BEST FRIEND READ-ALOUD

All the Places to Love, written by Patricia MacLachlan and illustrated by Mike Wimmer

Let's consider how signals in the text might impact our delivery of the music in language when we read aloud. To do this, let's contrast the opening lines of two picture books, *All the Places to Love* and *The Recess Queen*.

TONE

The overall tone of this read-aloud is gentle and caring.

INTENSITY

Energy in this book is steady and flowing. It is smooth and silky.

PACING

The pace matches the energy and is a gentle, flowing stream of beautiful language. This book should not be rushed.

MOOD

The general mood of this book is peaceful, graceful, kind, and loving.

All the Places to Love, with art by Mike Wimmer, begins with one sentence placed on the page in three phrases:

On the day I was born

My grandmother wrapped me in a blanket

made from the wool of her sheep.

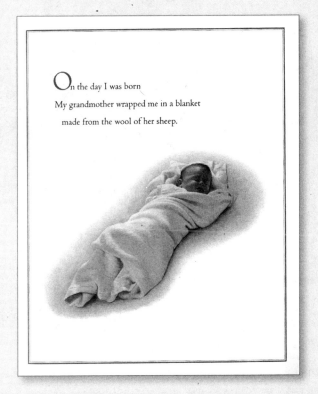

The second page presents the language so that each line begins with a capital letter (as in some poetry), and the line breaks on the right indicate a slow, deliberate pace and a natural place to pause in the sound of language. Note also that these six lines are actually two sentences, and the second sentence ends with a list of three items, indicating a pause after each item in the list:

She held me up in the open window

So that what I heard first was the wind.

What I saw first were all the places to love:

The valley,

The river falling down over rocks,

The hilltop where the blueberries grew.

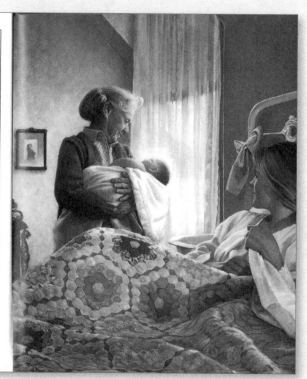

She held me up in the open window
So that what I heard first was the wind.
What I saw first were all the places to love:
The valley,
The river falling down over rocks.
The hilltop where the blueberries grew.

The placement of words, the line breaks, and the use of white space signal a slow, deliberate pace. As I see it, the pacing is established by phrasing that is set up in the line breaks. A slight pause is suggested at the end of each line, just as in the lines of poetry. To get a feel for the difference in the sound of it, try reading the above lines as if they were in a paragraph:

> **On the day I was born [m]y grandmother wrapped me in a blanket made from the wool of her sheep. She held me up in the open window [s]o that what I heard first was the wind. What I saw first were all the places to love: [t]he valley, [t]he river falling down over rocks, [t]he hilltop where the blueberries grew.**

To read this beautiful, fluid language in a rush is to rob the listener of its music. Reading it in a paragraph without the line breaks, without the pauses, creates a sense of moving through at a steady pace until you reach an end punctuation mark. It would be somewhat like playing music too fast: you lose something beautiful, something pleasing to the ear. Presenting the language in phrases, with the line breaks in place, suggests the pauses that create that small silence between thoughts. Those small, silent spaces offer the brain an opportunity to process each bit of information, layering it into a unified message.

Consider this:

On the day I was born	[Slight pause.]
My grandmother wrapped me in a blanket	[Slight pause.]
made from the wool of her sheep.	[Full stop.]
She held me up in the open window	[Slight pause.]
So that what I heard first was the wind.	[Full stop.]
What I saw first were all the places to love:	[Long pause.]
The valley,	[Slight pause.]
The river falling down over rocks,	[Slight pause.]
The hilltop where the blueberries grew.	[Full stop.]

Now try reading it aloud. Listen to your own voice and try to shift the pacing as indicated above. Try it two or three times until you find a rhythm that sounds natural and sounds as if you are presenting something of value in each line. Contrast that with a reading of the paragraph format presented before.

What you notice is the music in the language. It's a rhythm that will tease the ear and engage the mind of listeners when you read aloud and attend to the *sound print* of the writer's voice. We talk about style and voice when we teach our students to write. In writer's workshop and when conferring, we help children find their own voices by studying the voices of other writers. That is part of using picture books as mentor texts and part of the work we do in the study of craft. Through artful read-alouds, we can help children learn to arrest the rhythm of language with their ears, but that will only happen if we are playing the music of that language on the instrument of our voices (to take that music analogy a bit further).

When I read a picture book, I also notice the art, as it helps me interpret the tone of the book. The first page of *All the Places to Love* is a tender image in gentle tones depicting a newborn baby wrapped in a soft, cream-colored blanket. The image is realistic, almost like a portrait or a photograph. This tender image immediately suggests a soft tone. It is as if the writer and the illustrator are signaling the reader to speak quietly (to let this little baby sleep) in much the same way a composer would signal the musician with *p (piano)*, indicating the intention to play softly, quietly.

So in the opening pages of most any book there are signals to suggest how the reader might deliver the text. We see signals in the line breaks and punctuation and in the spacing and placement of phrases. We also see signals in the palate of color, in the style of the art, and in images themselves. As readers who will deliver the text to listeners, we can make the whole event more robust and more memorable if we attend to those signals.

The Recess Queen, written by Alexis O'Neill and illustrated by Laura Huliska-Beith

Let's contrast the signals in a quiet, tender story like *All the Places to Love* with the story of a playground bully. In *The Recess Queen* by Alexis O'Neill, with art by Laura Huliska-Beith, we meet a young girl who is a playground bully.

TONE

The overall tone of this read-aloud is bright, quick, a bit aggressive, with a shift at the end toward friendship.

INTENSITY

Energy runs high in this read-aloud. Your voice will need to reflect the high energy of a playground and translate the emotions at play.

PACING

The pace matches the energy and the quick pulse of moving across a crowded playground.

MOOD

The general mood of this book is humorous, yet the subject is more serious.

The opening lines on the first spread present the bully:

MEAN JEAN was Recess Queen

and nobody said any different.

This first sentence is presented on two lines, again suggesting a particular emphasis. The first line establishes Mean Jean's identity. The second line makes it clear that her identity is unchallenged.

The next page (opposing page on the same spread) presents three sentences that are listed as three separate statements rather than written in paragraph form:

Nobody swung until Mean Jean swung.

Nobody kicked until Mean Jean kicked.

Nobody bounced until Mean Jean bounced.

The language is presented in phrases, just as in *All the Places to Love*. Does that suggest a slow, deliberate pace? Not to me. Note that the first two words in the first sentence are in a different font, all capital letters and in bold print—"**MEAN JEAN**." That suggests a strong voice, a bold beginning, as if the composer is signaling the musician to begin with an *ff* (*fortissimo* or very loud). We open with intensity that helps establish the identity of the main character and sets the tone of dominance that a bully works so hard to create. As we continue, the language is presented in a bold, clear, tight font that is unembellished, suggesting to me that we are to keep that tone present as we read.

Let's examine how the presentation of the language actually makes a difference in how we make it sound when we read aloud. By way of contrast, try reading this opening, written in paragraph form, with a more traditional font, and without the use of capital letters at the beginning of the sentence. It would look like this:

Mean Jean was Recess Queen and nobody said any different.

Nobody swung until Mean Jean swung. Nobody kicked until

Mean Jean kicked. Nobody bounced until Mean Jean bounced.

So just read it aloud a few times as if you are reading a paragraph. Of course, if you have read the book aloud many times, you may be influenced by your attention to the features of the print and the presentation of the art. So try to divorce your mind from those influences. Just read the sentences in the paragraph as if you were the anchor on the six o'clock news. . . . It sounds flat, doesn't it? And you certainly don't leave with a highly emotional response to Jean.

Now let's layer the format back into the presentation. I'll change the font to simulate the presentation in the book:

MEAN JEAN was Recess Queen

and nobody said any different.

Nobody swung until Mean Jean swung.

Nobody kicked until Mean Jean kicked.

Nobody bounced until Mean Jean bounced.

Wow, what a difference that makes! Clearly, this will not sound like the anchor on the six o'clock news. Nor will it have the quiet, tender tone of *All the Places to Love*. This bold print, the enlarged font, and the line breaks suggest something more for me. Consider the following suggestions. Note how the bold print, the selection of font, and the subject (bullying) lead you toward a sense of defiance, a strong voice, a louder voice:

MEAN JEAN was Recess Queen	[Bold voice to establish her role.]
and nobody said any different.	[Defiant tone, dare anyone to challenge.]

On the next page (opposing page of the same spread), note how the sentences are presented in a list, making the parallel structure quite visible. This creates a listing effect, as if you are making the rules quite clear. It is also introducing the main character and establishing her role as playground bully. That personality is more evident in this presentation:

Nobody swung until Mean Jean swung.	[Bold, defiant voice; full stop.]
Nobody kicked until Mean Jean kicked.	[Bold, defiant voice; full stop.]
Nobody bounced until Mean Jean bounced.	[Bold, defiant voice; full stop.]

When I consider the art, I have even more signals for interpreting the sound of this book. The illustrations are rendered in bold and bright acrylic and collage, giving the book a strong and vivid look. The opening spread makes a clear statement, with Mean Jean consuming practically all of the first page. Her arms are crossed, her body is leaning in toward the center of the page, and her head is the largest feature on the spread. Her face has a snarky, satisfied grimace and her eyes glare across the spread into a crowd of children clustered somewhat like bowling pins. The faces of the children are wide-eyed, with mouths drawn in tight little O's as they await the signal from Mean Jean letting them know they have her permission to play. The bold color, paired with a perspective that presents a sharp contrast between the size of Jean and the other children, creates a defiant, bold, bullying tone that is supported by the features in the print. These features could create an aggressive feel, but are abated somewhat by the animated style of illustration.

WHEN PREPARING FOR A READ-ALOUD EXPERIENCE:

- Consider the artwork: do the colors suggest a bold, boisterous voice or a quiet, more subdued tone; is there movement and energy calling for a more rapid pace and greater intensity, or is the art more static and peaceful, calling for a slower, softer voice?

- Read the dedication yourself and share it with your students if there is additional insight offered there—the dedication can offer a window into the author's motives and connections to the text.

- Examine the endpapers—these often carry a motif or design from the text, giving insight into a theme or feeling for the book that can influence your presentation of the language.

- Consider the genre and what you know and expect from texts written in that genre—a biography would be read with different emphasis than humor or poetry, for example.

- Review the author and illustrator information on the flap—this information can provide insight into the influences in the writing or illustration style, topic, and presentation.

- Preview the book by reading it aloud to yourself ahead of time; listen for the rhythm and find the flow.

- Read the book at least once silently and then once aloud to find the rhythm and note the points in the text where you might need to pause or quicken the pace, drop your voice to a whisper, or build to a near shout.

- Note those places in the text where you may need to pause for a brief comment or scaffold meaning for the audience—avoid overdoing this, and be careful to recognize that it isn't necessary in every book.

- Change the tone of your voice to match the dialogue or the personality of the characters, or to set the mood when possible.

- Adjust your pace to fit the story, slowing down for dramatic pauses and speeding up to create movement and energy.

- Make your voice expressive; convey the emotional quality of the text.

- Know why you are presenting a particular text; be clear about your expectations of the book, your presentation, and the students— let this information guide your voice as it conveys tone and mood through pacing and intensity.

- Position yourself so that both you and the children are comfortable, your voice can carry to the entire group, and the illustrations (if there are any) can be seen.

- Vary the length and subject matter of the read-aloud experience. Include picture books, storybooks, chapter books, nonfiction, and poetry.

- Allow your listeners a few minutes to settle down and adjust their bodies and minds to the story.

- Allow time for (but don't require) discussion after reading.

- Add a third dimension to the book when it will add depth and enhance the experience—for example, bring a bowl of blueberries to be eaten after reading Robert McCloskey's *Blueberries for Sal.*

"*Powerful writers and powerful speakers have two wells they can draw on for that power: one is the well of rhythm; the other is the well of vocabulary. But vocabulary and a sense of rhythm are almost impossible to 'teach' in the narrow sense of the word. So how are children to develop a sense of rhythm or a wide vocabulary? By being read to, aloud, a lot!*"

—MEM FOX

Diary of a Worm, written by Doreen Cronin and illustrated by Harry Bliss

Now let's consider a book that is clearly intended as humor, Doreen Cronin's *Diary of a Worm*, with illustrations by Harry Bliss. Just take a look at the cover. There's a worm with a ball cap on his head, holding a pencil with his tail, "sitting" on a bottle cap, and using a mushroom as his desk while writing intently in an open notebook. Who could take this seriously? I know immediately I am going to have fun with this one. The title, in large orange print, is presented in all capitals. That captures my attention. The endpapers of this book present a scrapbook of our cover character and his friends, family, and mementos.

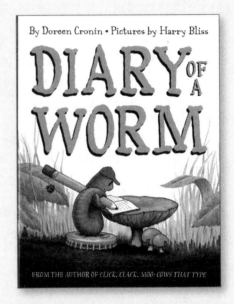

Open the book to any spread and you will see a diary format. There is a date printed in the upper left corner of the page with a narrative capturing an event of that day. Of course, being a diary written by a worm, it is told from a worm's point of view. Therefore, the entire book is filled with "worm humor." All this just layers in the humor and suggests a lighthearted tone that should be reflected in your voice.

TONE

The overall tone of this read-aloud is light, easy, and fun.

INTENSITY

Energy shifts very little throughout the reading of this text. There are places where you drop your voice to show a shift in the emotional tone.

PACING

Overall, the pace of this read-aloud is rather steady. There are places where pauses are necessary to deliver the "punchline." In those places, silence is actually helpful, as it draws attention to the shift.

MOOD

The general mood of this book is upbeat, light-hearted, and humorous with a positive feeling.

Turn to the spread for May 28. Notice that the print is presented with a good bit of space between each idea. There is a small illustration under each cluster of print (four illustrations in all; two on the left page and two on the right). In each of the illustrations we see the "heads and shoulders" of six worms in various leaning positions.

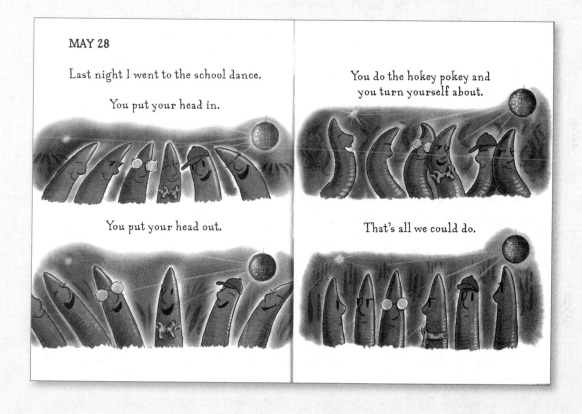

The text reads:

MAY 28

Last night I went to the school dance.
       You put your head in.
[Illustration shows six worms from the "waist" up, all leaning in.]

You put your head out.
[Illustration shows six worms, all leaning out.]

You do the hokey pokey and
       you turn yourself about.
[Illustration shows six worms rotating.]

That's all we could do.
[Illustration shows six worms standing straight with solemn faces.]

One quick read and you know this is a childhood song with actions. A quick glance at the four illustrations and you recognize the worms are doing the hokey pokey. Recognizing this childhood favorite calls for you to sing the second, third, fourth, and fifth lines.

Try this. Read the brief text as if you are that news anchor again. I'll collapse the text for you to see it as a paragraph:

May 28 Last night I went to the school dance. You put your head in. You put your head out. You do the hokey pokey and you turn yourself about. That's all we could do.

To read this as if it were the news renders something that sounds like a bad farce, a *Saturday Night Live* skit gone bad. If we read it with our attention given to accuracy (getting all the words right) and rate (reading it quickly) and don't attend to the music of the language, we get something that sounds less like language and more like nonsense. The humor is lost. The meaning diminishes and the whole effect is deflated.

To understand the music of language, we have to pay attention to other signals in the print, in the layout, in the art, and in the language itself. We have to interpret as we read, make sense of the situation, and let our use of pacing, tone, intensity, and mood reflect those decisions. Looking at the book pages at top, let's examine those signals.

The art is whimsical, almost comedic. The expressions and movement of the worms suggest frivolity in the first three scenes and a deadpan solemnity in the final scene.

The language blends a narrative and lyrics from a song. The spacing suggests four quick and successive scenes recording one event.

This time, try reading it as if you were telling a friend about the evening:

MAY 28

Last night I went to the school dance.

[Read like you are telling a friend what you did last night. If you went to a dance you probably were excited. Let your voice show that.]

You put your head in.

[Sing the first line of the familiar song. Slight pause.]

You put your head out.

[Sing the second line. Slight pause.]

You do the hokey pokey and you turn yourself about.

[Sing the third and fourth lines. Full stop. Let there be some silence before the next line.]

That's all we could do.

[Stand still. Drop all expression from your face and deliver this last line in a very solemn tone.]

Next, let's take a look at the April 10 entry to see how pacing can further influence the power of the read-aloud:

APRIL 10

It rained all night and the ground

was soaked. We spent the entire day

on the sidewalk.

Hopscotch is a very dangerous game.

APRIL 10

It rained all night and the ground was soaked. We spent the entire day on the sidewalk.

Hopscotch is a very dangerous game.

When looking at a read-aloud, I take signals for pacing from the use of white space, line breaks, and the rhythm in the language itself. In this example, I can't rely on the line breaks for a sense of pacing because they are determined by the size of the page. In other words, each line runs to the end of the page and returns when the margin is reached. So there does not appear to be any deliberate attempt to influence the pace with an intentional line break.

So next, I look to the language for cues. These three sentences are presenting four ideas:

1. It rained all night.

2. The ground was soaked.

3. We spent all day on the sidewalk.

4. Hopscotch is a dangerous game.

So to make sure the listeners get all four ideas as I read, I will pause slightly after each idea. I do that in an effort to help my audience build and layer an understanding. As you look back to the text you will see that the first section ends with the word *sidewalk*. Then there is an extra line space before the next sentence, as if adding another paragraph. Note the four ideas presented. The first three are connected to explain why the worm family spent a day on the sidewalk. It is something like the setup in a joke. The fourth idea, that hopscotch is dangerous, is only funny if you think about it from the worm's perspective.

A long pause between the third idea and the fourth allows the audience to create a scene, see the rain soaking into the ground, flooding little worm homes, and to imagine the worms moving up and out to safety. That image has to settle before you drop the idea about hopscotch, or the two will not connect.

Try this out. I'll present the exact language, but I'll reformat it so that it appears as one block of text:

APRIL 10

It rained all night and the ground

was soaked. We spent the entire day

on the sidewalk. Hopscotch is a very

dangerous game.

Now read it as if you were reading a paragraph. Read with no pauses beyond what you would normally layer in for a period. Read it aloud two or three times, trying to keep the pace even. Do you notice how the last idea seems out of place without that long pause?

Try one more thing. Let's attend to tone and intensity this time. The overall tone is light and fun. The intensity (energy, pitch, passion) is moderate. There is a shift in tone between the third idea and the fourth one. The tone of the first three ideas (the first two sentences) is a somewhat neutral reporting of fact, so the intensity would be lessened here. If it were music, we might see an *mf (mezzo forte)* notation written in beneath the music.

APRIL 10

It rained all night and the ground

was soaked. We spent the entire day

on the sidewalk.

Hopscotch is a very dangerous game.

But that line space signals a rest, a full-measure rest. So after reading the first two sentences in a neutral tone (not anxious, not eager, not worried), allow a long pause. That bit of silence builds tension, layers suspense, and, most importantly, allows the audience to process the three ideas in those first two sentences. Now drop the last idea, the third sentence, on them. *Drop* is the appropriate term here. I actually drop my voice, lower my tone, stepping out of that neutral tone and into a more somber, more worried tone of voice to read the final sentence. That shift creates a contrast that spikes the humor in the passage.

Snow Day! written by Lester L. Laminack and illustrated by Adam Gustavson

Intensity in the read-aloud can be examined with *Snow Day!* by Lester L. Laminack. This book (yes, I wrote it) is a story of anticipation—living through those hours between the weatherman's prediction for significant snowfall and the morning after. The intensity or energy in this book is evident from the first line and continues at a high level to the last line.

TONE

The overall tone of this read-aloud is jovial, fun.

INTENSITY

Energy begins high and remains high.

PACING

Overall, the pace of this read-aloud is rather steady. It moves at a quick clip that reflects the high energy of the text.

MOOD

The general mood of this book is eager anticipation, leaving the reader with a positive, upbeat feeling.

SPOTLIGHT ON LESTER VIDEO

Lester Reads *Snow Day!* by Lester L. Laminack

scholastic.com/BFBresources

Let's step inside:

Did you *hear* that?

Did the weatherman just say what I

thought he did?

Did he say…

SNOW?

Oh please, let it snow. Lots and lots of snow.

First notice the short sentences dancing back and forth on the page. Notice the word *snow* popping out at you. This is the announcement that snow is on the way. That builds energy and anticipation in most households with school-age children (or at least one teacher). That energy calls for intensity in your voice when you read aloud.

Imagine reading this aloud to your students as if you were that six o'clock news anchor:

> **Did you hear that? Did that weatherman just say what I thought he did? Did he say . . . SNOW? Oh please, let it snow. Lots and lots of snow.**

Even this presentation of the print zaps energy from this much-anticipated event. Consider it again in the original form:

Did you *hear* that?

[The narrator is speaking directly to you. Notice the italics used for emphasis, nudging you to punch up the intensity there.]

Did the weatherman just say what I thought he did?

[Notice the space between the first line and this one, signaling you to pause. It's as if you are waiting to hear from the weatherman again. Your voice calls to the listener to confirm what you heard, engaging the audience.]

Did he say . . .

[Notice the hesitation, the trailing off marked by the ellipses.]

SNOW?

[How could you miss this cue? Notice the enlarged font, the use of all capitals, and bold print begging you to significantly increase the intensity.]

Oh please, let it snow.
Lots and lots of snow.

[This is a plea. Let your voice plead with the audience.]

In this presentation, the placement of text, the use of font size and italics and bold, the series of three questions, and a plea all work together to build the energy of a possible snowfall and the hope for a snow day. So when you read it aloud, the intensity of your voice should reflect that energy, leaving the audience with that sense of eager anticipation.

MY FAVORITE WAYS TO INTRODUCE A BOOK

1. PICTURE WALK

2. BOOK TALK/COMMERCIAL

3. AUTHOR PROFILE

4. THEME/TOPIC LINK

5. JUST START READING

Picture Walk

Today we are going to read this book [hold the book so the front cover is visible]. It is called *Snow Day!* The author is Lester Laminack, and the illustrator is Adam Gustavson. Take a look at the illustration on the front. These two kids seem to be zipping down a hill on this red sled. Before we read this one, let's take a walk through the pictures and see what is going on. Turn to the first illustration and begin a conversation. It may go something like what follows: Well, I see a boy looking right at us and his eyes are really large. He looks excited. I wonder what he might be excited about. And look at the girl lying there on the floor in front of the TV. Mmmm, that's interesting, the man on the TV is standing in front of a map and that looks like clouds and snowflakes. I wonder what that man is talking about. Oh look, there is one more person in the illustration. See the man over here? He looks like a grown-up, and he's wearing an apron and has a spatula in his hand. It looks as if he is coming from the kitchen to see what is going on. Now I'm really wondering what these three are talking about. Let's turn the page and take a look at the next illustration, shall we?

HOME VISIT

Help Students Introduce Best Friend Books to Families

scholastic.com/BFBresources

At school, students learned multiple ways to introduce a Best Friend Book. Now invite them to introduce their BFBs to their families. Consider making videos of students introducing their Best Friend Books to share at home.

Book Talk/Commercial

Just imagine how excited you'd feel if you heard the TV weatherperson announce the possibility of a big snowfall on a *SCHOOL NIGHT!* Imagine what you'd be thinking about and how excited you would get. Perhaps you'd be thinking about staying up late to watch TV. Or sleeping in the next morning. Or you might be thinking about your homework and how you could just skip it until the next day. Maybe you'd be thinking about all the fun you could have spending the day playing in the snow—snow forts and snowball fights, sledding and snowmen. ... Oh, and then you'd need to come inside and get warm. There's bound to be hot chocolate on a snow day—mmmm, I do love a good mug full of hot chocolate. Today we are reading *Snow Day!* I can hardly wait, let's get right to it and see what happens on this snow day. ...

Author Profile

Today I have a new book for us. This one is called *Snow Day!*, and look, it's written by Lester Laminack. We know who that is. He wrote *Saturdays and Teacakes*. He also wrote a few other books that we have in our room; do you remember which books he wrote? Let's take a look [have the books close by and hold each one up]. He wrote *Jake's 100th Day of School* and *Trevor's Wiggly-Wobbly Tooth*. Those stories remind us of the things we do at school. We have talked about that several times. He also wrote *The Sunsets of Miss Olivia Wiggins*; remember how that one always makes me cry because it reminds me of my grandmother? And he wrote one of our favorites, *Three Hens and a Peacock*. I checked Lester's website and bookmarked the page for you if you'd like to go there for yourself. I discovered that Lester was a teacher in an elementary school and in a university. That helps us understand why he might write about what happens at school in *Trevor's Wiggly-Wobbly Tooth* and *Jake's 100th Day of School*. I'm thinking *Snow Day!* might have a connection to school as well. Let's try to remember to look for that as we read. I also found out that he grew up in a very small Alabama town called Heflin. And I discovered that *Saturdays and Teacakes* is a memoir about growing up in that small town. I am wondering if there is anything from his life in this book, *Snow Day!* Let's think about that when we are listening. Remind me to check the dedication, since authors sometimes share connections for us there. And one more thing I discovered when reading about Lester. He lives in Asheville, North Carolina, and it does snow there in winter. So now I'm wondering if that's where he got the idea for this new book. Let's take a look inside and see what we find.

Theme/Topic Link

Sometimes unexpected things can make us change our plans. Rainstorms can cause us to cancel soccer practice. A flat tire on a bike can make us walk when we planned to ride. Sometimes we expect something in the mail and it takes a week longer to arrive than we thought it would. A delay at the airport can cause us to miss a trip. Unexpected events can make us change our plans, and that is what we are reading about this week. I have a basket of books here, and we will read one each day. These are stories about all kinds of plans that just don't work out because something unexpected happens. Let's take a look at the first one, *Snow Day!*, written by Lester Laminack with illustrations by Adam Gustavson. Take a moment before we begin to read; let's think about what unexpected event may make these characters change their plans. What plans do you suppose they had? [At this point I sometimes have students share their thinking with someone near first, then share out.] Let's settle in and see what goes awry in this story. . . .

Just Start Reading

Well, duh . . . this is pretty clear, huh? All kidding aside, I often just share the title, author, and illustrator, then begin.

Stepping Back to Consider Our Intentions

When you next launch a read-aloud experience in your classroom, think about your intentions. Are you reading aloud to *inspire* your students to become readers and writers? Are you trying to have them fall in love with a genre, topic, title, author, or illustrator? Or is the experience an *investment* in the development of their language and understandings? Are you building background for future instruction? Or will you be reading aloud to them at the point of *instruction*? Will you select the text you read for the purpose of teaching them something? Will this text build off the previous ones? Will it be grounded in a unit of study in a subject area?

Whatever your intentions when you next read aloud, think about setting the stage to maximize the effect. Our students thrive on structure and routine, so the read-aloud experience should be a consistent event. You can find very specific suggestions for six opportunities for reading aloud across a single day in *Learning Under the Influence of Language and Literature* (Laminack & Wadsworth, 2006). In that book, Reba Wadsworth and I suggest six different times in the typical school day when teachers could insert a read-aloud. In addition, we offer a very specific purpose for each of them. You will also find more than 400 picture books listed out, annotated, and organized by purpose. Having a designated time and purpose is important. It is also important to set the stage in other ways.

- **Physical setting**—have a consistent location from which you will read. If the audience is seated in chairs, I like sitting on a tall stool while reading aloud. Otherwise, I prefer to sit on the floor, with my audience gathered close enough to see the illustrations.

- **Select a location that makes the book visible** without having the glare of a window behind you, and avoid sitting in a position that causes the audience to have to look up the entire time.

- **Establish an atmosphere in the classroom that supports engagement** in the read-aloud experience. Clear other materials and work away. Make yourself and the text the focal point. Eliminate distractions or reduce them to a minimum.

- **Introduce the text you are presenting in the read-aloud**—show the cover and announce the title, author, and illustrator. Invite the students to examine the cover art. Read the flap copy regarding the text and the brief profile of the author and illustrator. Read the dedication. Examine the endpapers and do a brief picture walk through the book if it is a picture book. Lead the students to use the information garnered to make predictions about the text.

- **Introduce the read-aloud experience by stating your purpose:** "Today as I read I'd like you to be thinking about . . . ," or "I selected this text for read-aloud today because it will help us understand what was going on during the days when Anne Frank was a little girl. . . . "

- **If your intentions for the read-aloud experience warrant it, draw attention to specific features of the text,** such as text boxes, charts, sidebars, graphs, captions, labels, bold type, font type shifts, font size shifts, diagrams, the index, appendices, and so on.

- **If your intentions warrant it, pause at critical junctures** to raise questions in students' minds.

WHAT THE RESEARCH SAYS

Wasik and Bond (2001) investigated the learning potential of the interactive read-aloud. Their study, which included 121 four-year-old children from low-income families (94 percent of whom were African American), engaged the treatment group in interactive book reading. This included defining vocabulary words, providing opportunities for children to use words from the books, asking open-ended questions, and giving children a chance to talk and be heard. The control teachers received all the books that the treatment teachers did and read the books as often in their control classrooms as the treatment teachers read in their classrooms; however, control teachers did not receive the interactive read-aloud training that treatment teachers received.

For the first four weeks of the intervention, an experienced teacher modeled the interactive book reading techniques in each treatment classroom. Then, for the next 11 weeks, treatment teachers ran the program on their own. At post-test, treatment classes scored significantly higher on the Peabody Picture Vocabulary than control classes did. Treatment classes also scored significantly higher on their knowledge of target vocabulary words, perhaps in part because treatment teachers were significantly more likely to use the target words during related activities.

Closing Thoughts

Read-alouds, when done well, are like a storytelling performance. The reader must take the time necessary to preview and rehearse the book, just as a storyteller would. The voice is the instrument that brings life to the language of the writer and that voice has to convey the tone of the characters and the narrator, the emotion of the scene, and the mood of the situation. We cannot reasonably expect that our students will hear those features of a story in their own minds unless we provide a demonstration for what is possible. We are the models for how fluency works—how written language flows into sound with the potential to lift meaning. We set examples for how a character's personality influences tone, and how emotions influence intensity. We demonstrate how the voice conveys mood. Reading aloud is no frivolous activity; it is solid instructional work when our intentions are clear.

CHAPTER 7

Some Ideas for Best Friend Books
(and Why I Love Them)

> *"Whether we are called upon to govern a nation or organize a birthday party for too many children, the key to both surviving our days and cultivating our next generation of leaders is many books, well chosen."*
>
> **—KYLE ZIMMER, DIRECTOR OF FIRST BOOK**

I love reading aloud for kids (and adults). I find pleasure in discovering another wonderful book that will be a hit as a read-aloud and then playing with it until I have the performance ready. I have my standard read-aloud books that I count on time and time again. I have books that I have used in read-aloud experiences or performances for years. If you love reading aloud, if you fall into the book and live there for a few moments and become part of the whole experience, then you know what I mean. Like any of you who love books, I find it agonizing to make a list of favorites. While I sit here typing I am in a space surrounded by nearly 3,000 picture books that are my personal property. So if you stop me at a workshop or at a conference and ask what my favorite books are, I'll have to say, "Well, at the moment I'm enamored with. …" This list represents books that I have returned to across time. I'm guessing you have your favorites, too. Well, just imagine the list we could amass if we began sharing our lists of standards. I'll go first.

All the Places to Love
by Patricia MacLachlan

I adore the lush, fluid river of language flowing through the writing of Patricia MacLachlan. This is my favorite of her many books. I love the gentle rhythm and the soft, tender feelings of love and respect this narrator has for his family.

Apt. 3 by Ezra Jack Keats

I have deep admiration for the work of Ezra Jack Keats. He honors the child and the universal experiences of childhood. I aspire to his clarity and his ability to capture those magical moments of childhood in a timeless way. *Apt. 3* is masterful. The use of detail, the integral role of the setting, and the nicely developed characters make this a gem.

The Barn Owls by Tony Johnston

Tony Johnston is a writer whose work I have long admired. Of all her many books, this is one of my two favorites. It is a sensory feast with attention to small details used to build a sense of the cycle of life, and it has a respect for nature, traditions, and place. I love reading this one aloud. It drips slowly off the tongue like raindrops from leaves.

HOME VISIT

Help Families Create Their Own BFB Collection
scholastic.com/BFBresources

Invite families to watch Lester explain how he chooses Best Friend Books. As Lester reminds them, "levels" belong at school, not at home. Check the online Home Visit section for videos that can be used with families along with a URL you can provide for easy access. You can also share these videos at a Family Literacy Event or Back-to-School Night.

Birmingham, 1963 by Carole Boston Weatherford

I am drawn to stories that deliver deep, powerful, and thought-provoking concepts with the elegance of simplicity. Carole Weatherford does that time and again. Here we have a fictionalized account of a young girl's tenth birthday with the excitement of her Youth Day solo at church woven into the fibers of history. The story takes place on that actual Sunday in September 1963 when four little girls lost their lives in the bombing of the Sixteenth Street Baptist Church in Birmingham, Alabama.

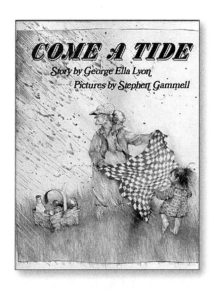

Come a Tide by George Ella Lyon

George Ella has an exquisite ear for capturing the language of the people of rural Appalachia. This story gives us an opportunity to listen to the music of that language and to deepen our understanding of the bonds of family and neighbors in a life of a bygone era.

Each Kindness by Jacqueline Woodson

I am a fan of Jackie Woodson. It is that simple. I admire her language and the graceful, elegant way she is able to take on tough topics. Jackie allows us to see the unkindness, the growing self-awareness, the reflection, and the regret within Chloe across the arc of this story.

In November by Cynthia Rylant

I love the beautiful descriptions, the sensory detail, and the music of this book. It aptly captures the warmth and love of friends and family gathering in this special time of year. I count on Cynthia Rylant to capture the people, the language, and the sense of place when she writes of home.

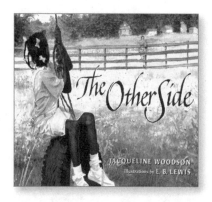

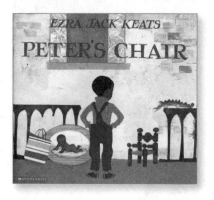

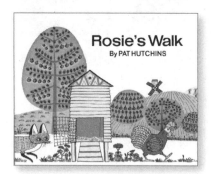

Koala Lou by Mem Fox

Long ago, Mem Fox stole my heart. I fell in love with her words. She is a master of rhythm and queen of big messages in small packages. I adore this book because the read-aloud is like music and the message is tuned to my heart.

The Other Side by Jacqueline Woodson

Jacqueline Woodson is one of those writers who is willing to take on the tough issues in the lives of children. She consistently does it with grace and eloquence. I love how this book captures the innocence of children—their open minds and accepting hearts—even when the adults around them are frozen by fear and distrust, which breed hatred. The rhythm and flow of this one makes it a pleasure to share as a read-aloud.

Peter's Chair by Ezra Jack Keats

This simple text has a tight focus that allows us to think about Peter as a real character. We see him react to his emotions, explore options, reflect, and arrive at a logical solution on his own. I admire the work Ezra Jack Keats for so many reasons.

Rosie's Walk by Pat Hutchins

Okay, I know this one has been around a long time, but there are timeless qualities about this book that bring me back to it again and again. The language is so very simple and speaks only to what Rosie does on her walk. But it is the Fox's story that children always dig into, and we have to bring our story language to the art for that one.

Saturdays and Teacakes
by Lester L. Laminack

My own memoir and, I think, my best writing thus far. I love reading this aloud because I know the music by heart in this tribute to my maternal grandmother. A book holds the potential to take you into the life of the author and the life of the reader all at once. I aimed for that in this book.

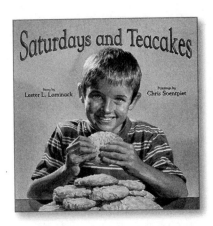

Scarecrow by Cynthia Rylant

I love the use of repeated lines, building up and layering meaning, giving life and emotion to a common scarecrow with such attention to the small details that matter. Exquisite. A wonderful, slow-paced feast for the reader and the listener.

Seven Blind Mice by Ed Young

This is a favorite because it has the potential to mean more and more each time you visit. It has a nice storytelling quality with parallel details that layer over the story. I adore the play on color and the gender twist with White Mouse. It is a book you'll want to read over and over as you discover new and different meanings.

Three Hens and a Peacock
by Lester L. Laminack

Yes, I know I wrote it. Yes, I know it seems self-serving, but I would love this book even if I were not the author. It is fun. I delight in becoming the hens with their sassy, snarky, fit of jealousy. I adore stepping into the role of the confused peacock trying to find his way. And I enjoy taking on the role of the tired, old hound who only wants some peace and quiet to return to.

Twilight Comes Twice by Ralph Fletcher

Ralph captures the magic of dawn and dusk in exquisite language. This book reads like a long poem and is peppered with metaphors and lyrical descriptions. If books were chocolate, this would be an exquisite, rich truffle.

Water Dance by Thomas Locker

I love reading this beautiful presentation of art. Locker's paintings are simply impeccable, and the writing here is art as well. I especially enjoy the water talking directly to the reader, identifying itself in all the forms water can take on its journey. It is poetry and music to read aloud.

What You Know First by Patricia MacLachlan

Patricia MacLachlan is one of my five favorite writers. I love her writing. It is a feast to read aloud, to listen to. This particular piece has beautiful repetitions and parallel structures that I adore. I never rush this one—as if I were enjoying a rich, expensive dark chocolate truffle. I relish every moment.

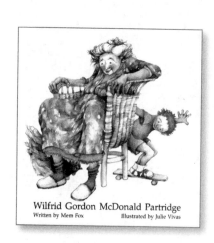

Wilfrid Gordon McDonald Partridge
Written by Mem Fox   Illustrated by Julie Vivas

Wilfrid Gordon McDonald Partridge by Mem Fox

I fell in love with Mem because of this book. It was one of the first books I read aloud so frequently that people actually brought it to me and asked that I sign their copy. I had to smile and say, I didn't write it, I just love it. I adore the tenderness, the love, and the innocence of a child captured here. I love the movement through the book, taking Wilfrid from person to person in search of understanding to help his dear friend. I love the opportunity to play with voices. I simply love this book and I adore Mem—so would you expect less?

Yo! Yes? by Chris Raschka

What a delight to read aloud. You get to be two personalities when you read this one aloud. I have actually stood on two chairs and moved from one to the other as I shifted between these two characters. (Don't look at me like that—try it!)

And a Few More on the Playful Side:

Bubba and Beau Go Night-Night
by Kathy Appelt

Oh my, how I love to read this book (and the other two Bubba and Beau books as well). It is such fun to step into the persona, pull out the accent from my repertoire of voices, and just cut loose.

Diary of a Worm by Doreen Cronin

I have three favorite scenes in this book. I have read it thousands of times (literally) to thousands of people (literally). I still laugh when I read my three favorite entries. This one is an opportunity to fine-tune the importance of pace and intensity and tone. Have fun with it.

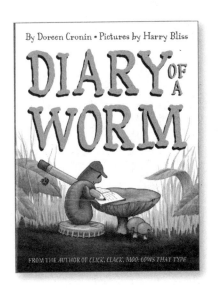

Epossumondas by Coleen Salley

I love Coleen. I love the music of her New Orleans–flavored voice. I love the personality that she exudes, and I try to capture the essence of that when I read this one aloud. I listen for Miss Coleen's pacing and slow down. I exaggerate and stretch words where I have heard her do it and take a few liberties of my own. I tap into my own rural Southern roots when I bring these words off the page.

Hungry Hen by Richard Waring

This one is a wonderful opportunity to explore the impact of pacing. Read this too quickly and you fail to allow the reader to build up the suspense, to anticipate and take delight in being right, or being shocked by the unexpected ending.

My Lucky Day by Keiko Kasza

The voice in this book is a treat to play with. Choose a voice for the piglet, who is feigning shock. Choose another for the fox, who is delighted to find dinner knocking at his door. Let your voice tease the listeners as they try to decide whose day is lucky.

The Recess Queen by Alexis O'Neill

Get an attitude. Let it rip. This book features a playground bully who meets her match in a teeny-tiny kid who is too new to understand the rules. Let your voice carry that attitude out to your listeners. Then everyone is surprised by the outcome.

Roller Coaster by Marla Frazee

Roller Coaster is a tight text capturing a moment in a big day at an amusement park. The focus of the book is on confronting the fears that come with a first ride on the roller coaster. The craft in the writing offers opportunities for the reader to play with pacing and intensity to build the tension associated with this event. Have fun when you read it.

Snow Day! by Lester L. Laminack

Yeah, I know, I wrote it and this looks like shameless self-promotion. But I love reading this one aloud. I crafted it to be a one-sided conversation where the narrator is speaking directly to you. I made decisions regarding line breaks, font changes, and punctuation to create the breathless energy of hoping for a snow day and frantically searching for all the essentials to make it great. The energy in the read-aloud should build, layering the imagination with greater and greater anticipation. And the ending should bring a smile.

Tanka Tanka Skunk! by Steve Webb

Okay, this is all about rhythm. Read it aloud a few times to find that beat, then try to read it with a few body movements. This can become a class favorite, so jump in there and let it rip.

The Three Armadillies Tuff by Jackie Mims Hopkins

So if you know me at all, if you have heard me read a few books aloud, you know that I can be a bit of a ham—just a tiny bit. Well, this book is a stage for a ham. There are four great characters in the three sisters and the coyote. You'll have a wonderful time cutting loose and stepping into the four personalities. When I read this I usually hear, "Read it again!"

Closing Thoughts

This collection of books represents an odd collection of topics and types of stories. There is a range of tone and mood represented here. These stories offer an opportunity to explore, to delve into different stories for various reasons as you find what works best for you and your students. Best Friend Books are special and have meaning that may be specific to you. Take your time to get to know a few books very well. Visit and revisit them again and again to find the nuances they offer your community of reader/writers. You may find it helpful to visit with these friends a few times as you discover where your best friends are likely to be hanging out.

Closing Comments and a Final Plea

"From that day forward, words and sentences and books, I discovered, when read and recited, could heal a tender heart."

—JUAN FELIPE HERRERA, POET LAUREATE

Most of us have had the experience of watching the same movie a second (or third) time. Most of us have viewed and viewed again (and perhaps again) the same episode of a favorite show on television. Even though we know what is going to happen, we watch again. We laugh again. We cry again. We are moved again. All of us have listened so often to a favorite song that we know the lyrics and sing along, perhaps we even sing in the shower without the music to accompany us.

WHAT THE RESEARCH SAYS

Anne Cunningham, renowned cognitive psychologist at the University of California, Berkeley, explains that reading is a "very rich, complex, and cognitive act" that offers an immense opportunity to exercise our intelligence in ways we lose if we don't read. Hundreds of correlated studies demonstrate that the most successful students read the most, while those who struggle read the least. These correlated studies suggest that the more our students read, the better their comprehension, vocabulary, and fluency—and the more likely they are to build a robust knowledge of the world. In short, reading provides us with a cognitive workout that transcends not only our inherent abstract problem-solving abilities, but also our levels of education. Reading makes us smart. (Cunningham, 2016)

When a story resonates with our hearts and minds, there is an inexplicable pull. The story (book, poem, article, movie, television program, song) lingers with us and we are drawn back to it. We need time to take it in because one visit didn't leave us satisfied. So we visit again, and perhaps again and again. There is something comforting about relishing the familiar that sets us up to notice the nuances we missed in first or second visits.

So it shouldn't surprise us that children want, if not need, the opportunity to visit with some stories again and again. Let us honor that need to get to know a few books intimately and hold them in our hearts and minds. Time spent reading aloud to children is never wasted. Let us slow the pace to unearth the nuances in language and art, in the actions and reactions of familiar characters, in the craft and technique and style of favorite authors, in the dialogue and narration of selected stories. Yes, I said let us slow the pace. I know the pressures are real—to do more, to cover more material, to push harder, and to do it all more quickly. I know the call to raise scores and achieve more. But we cannot lose sight of this truth: we are working with children. Honor the learner. Relish the learning. We are cultivating the hearts and minds of those who will lead this world in the years of our retirement. We are raising humans.

Humans need story. Story is how we make sense of our lives. Story helps us make sense of yesterday, navigate today, and imagine tomorrow. Story lets us see ourselves in a world larger than we can imagine on our own. Story lets us see others as a part of this one shared world, as members of this one human family. Story lets us imagine more. Story gives us a context, a frame of reference for considering the "what ifs" and "why nots" in life. Story helps us to be more, to outgrow our current selves, and to see beyond the horizon of our current circumstances. Story is essential to our existence.

It doesn't take much for us to imagine the benefits of having five thoughtfully selected stories in a classroom that become treasures in the hearts and minds of every single student. The investment of time to slow down and introduce each of the five books as new best friends is negligible. Those first visits are gifts of time, gifts of story, gifts of heart. And children know when a gift is given with a joyful heart. Knowing that you will visit again and again with a small collection of books removes the pressure to "strip mine" a beautiful story. Slowing down does not mean doing less. Rather, it means being more intentional, more focused, and more thoughtful about what you want your reader/writers to embrace and carry forward into their literate lives. Just imagine that while you confer with the readers and writers in your classroom, you know that each of them holds those same five stories in their hearts and heads. You know that you can refer to any scene in any of the five stories and each child will hold that reference in mind. Reading and writing with that knowledge "on deposit" puts us in a place where conversations about personal reading and writing share common connectors across the classroom community. So we read aloud. We read aloud with the zeal of a street performer and with the frequency of bird song. We read aloud knowing it matters. We read aloud with clear intentions and with focused instructional goals.

Bringing books into the community as new best friends operates on the assumption that we know those books intimately ourselves. It assumes we have read and reread

WHAT THE RESEARCH SAYS

The tangible rewards of reading aloud and discussing books with our children are both extensive and well grounded in research. Indeed, in l985, the federally funded Commission on Reading released a report entitled "Becoming a Nation of Readers" that stated: "The single most important activity for building the knowledge required for eventual success is reading aloud to children." (1985, p. 23)

those stories again and again, each time with a particular focus in mind. In other words, we have given ourselves the same experience that we are planning for our students because we understand that we cannot lead them where we have not traveled ourselves.

Take some time now to search through your books, to carefully and critically examine your schedule, to revisit your vision about why this matters. Pull a favorite book, stop what you are doing, and read to them.

Take time to read and reread the books in your collection to find those you can introduce as Best Friend Books. Slow down; give your students the pleasure of meeting a new character, exploring a new setting, facing a new challenge as you introduce them to your best friends. Slow down; take the time to let that first meeting be a gift you unwrap together without interruption. Know that you will revisit these friends again and again as you build deep and abiding relationships between your students and the love of literature.

> "When we read great books with our children, we teach them to turn to great books throughout their lives for comfort, humor, and for illumination of the human experience. The most influential leaders and thinkers in the world have consistently relied on literature for inspiration at their most difficult moments."
>
> ~KYLE ZIMMER,
> DIRECTOR OF FIRST BOOK

Friends, I urge you to reconnect to those stirrings that brought you into this profession. I urge you to refocus your attention to the children in your care. There is no more precious treasure in this world than the children of its people. Nothing holds greater potential for good, for truth, for justice than the children on this Earth.

In all things, be kind and truthful. Let nothing you do take from a child his or her dignity as a human being, his or her integrity as a learner, his or her identity as one who is capable. Cause no intentional harm.

Peace be with you.

References

Professional Resources

Beck, I. L., & Sandora, C., (2016). *Illuminating comprehension in close reading*. New York: Guilford Press.

Beck, I. L., & McKeown, M. G. (2001). Text talk: Capturing the benefits of read-aloud experiences for young children. *The Reading Teacher, 55*(1), 10–20.

Beers, K., & Probst, R. (2012). *Notice & note: strategies for close reading*. Portsmouth, NH: Heinemann.

Cambourne, B. (1988). *The whole story*. New York: Scholastic.

Cunningham, A. E., & Stanovich, K. E. (1998). What reading does for the mind. *American educator, 22*(1–2), 8–15.

Cunningham, A. E., & Zibulsky, J. (2013). *Book smart: How to develop and support successful, motivated readers*. New York: Oxford University Press.

Duke, N. (2014). *Inside information: Developing powerful readers and writers of informational text through project-based instruction*. New York: Scholastic.

Duke, N., Caughlan, S., Juzwik, M., & Martin, N. (2012). *Reading and writing genre with purpose in K–8 classrooms* (p. 5). Portsmouth, NH: Heinemann.

Duke, N., Pearson, D., Strachan, S., & Billman, A. (2011). "Essential elements of fostering and teaching reading comprehension." In J. Samuels & A. Farstrup (Eds.), What research has to say about reading instruction (fourth edition). Newark, DE: International Reading Association. Retrieved from: http://www.google.com/url?sa=t&rct= j&q=&esrc=s &source=web&cd=1&ved=0CB8QFjAA&url=http%3A%2F%2Fwww .literacyinlearningexchange.org%2Fsites%2Fdefault% 2Ffiles%2F03duke.pdf&ei=YdXvU53sEo3soA T8uIKgBA&usg=AFQjCNFGde_aD0trGt jnuW NN0GBd5zLDoA&bvm=bv.73231344,d.cGU

Fountas, I., & Pinnell, G. S. (2006) *Comprehending & fluency*. Portsmouth, NH: Heinemann.

Fox, M. (1993). *Radical reflections*. San Diego, CA: Harcourt.

Fox, M. (2001). *Reading magic*. San Diego, CA: Harcourt.

Halliday, M. A. K. (1973). *Explorations in the functions of language*. London: Edward Arnold.

Kintsch, W., & Rawson, K. A. (2005). Comprehension. In M. J. S. C. Hulme (Ed.), *The science of reading: a handbook*. Malden, MA: Blackwell Publishing (pp. 209–226).

Krashen, S. (2004). *The power of reading* (second edition). Portsmouth, NH: Heinemann Publishing Company, and Westview, CT: Libraries Unlimited.

Krashen, S. (2015). The great fiction/nonfiction debate. *Language Magazine*, November.

Laminack, L. L., & Wadsworth, R. M. (2006). *Learning under the influence of language and literature*. Portsmouth, NH: Heinemann.

Laminack, L. L., & Wadsworth, R. M. (2006). *Reading aloud across the curriculum*. Portsmouth, NH: Heinemann.

Pappano, L. (2015, February 4). Is your first grader college ready? *New York Times*. Retrieved from: http://www.nytimes.com/2015/02/08/education/edlife/is-your-first-grader-college-ready.html

Rasinski, T. (2010). *The fluent reader* (second edition). New York, Scholastic.

Roskos, K., & Neuman, S. (2014, April). Best practices in reading instruction: A 21st century skill update. *The Reading Teacher, 67*(7), 507–511.

Samuels, J. (1979, January). The method of repeated rereadings. *The reading teacher, 32*(4) 403–408.

Sanders, B. (1994). *A is for ox: The collapse of literacy and the rise of violence in an electronic age*. New York: Vintage Books.

Serafini, F. (2008). *Position statement: The vital role of picture books in the intermediate, middle and high school reading curriculum*.

Shefelbine, J., & Newman, K. K. (2004). *Sipps challenge assessment record book*. Oakland, CA: Developmental Studies Center.

Stanovich, K. E., & Cunningham, A. E. (1993). Where does knowledge come from? Specific associations between print exposure and information acquisition. *Journal of Educational Psychology, 85*(2), 211–229.

Wasik, B., & Bond, M. (2001). "The Effects of a Language and Literacy Intervention on Head Start Children and Teachers." Cited in Wasik, B. Bond, M. & Hindman, A. (Feb. 2006). *Journal of Educational Psychology*, Vol 98 (1), 63–74.

Children's Books

Ada, A. F. (2001). *Yours truly, Goldilocks*. New York: Aladdin.

Ada, A. F. (2004). *With love, Little Red Hen*. New York: Aladdin.

Ada, A. F. (2006). *Dear Peter Rabbit*. New York: Aladdin.

Appelt, K. (2003). *Bubba and Beau go night-night*. Orlando, FL: Harcourt Children's Books.

Bell-Rehwoldt, S. (2007). *You think it's easy being the tooth fairy?* San Francisco: Chronicle Books.

Cronin, D. (2003). *Diary of a worm*. New York: Joanna Cotler Books.

Dahl, R. (1998). *The BFG*. New York: Puffin Books.

Davies, N. (2004). *Bat loves the night*. Cambridge, MA: Candlewick.

Fletcher, R. (1997). *Twilight comes twice*. New York: Clarion Books.

Fox, M. (1985). *Wilfrid Gordon McDonald Partridge*. La Jolla, CA: Kane/Miller Book Publishers.

Fox, M. (1988). *Koala Lou*. Orlando, FL: Harcourt Children's Books.

Frazee, M. (2003). *Roller coaster*. San Diego, CA: Harcourt.

Gibbons, G. (2002). *Polar bears*. New York: Holiday House.

Gibbons, G. (2007). *Snakes*. New York: Holiday House.

Hopkins, J. M. (2002). *The three armadillies Tuff*. Atlanta: Peachtree.

Hutchins, P. (1971). *Rosie's walk*. New York: Aladdin.

Johnston, T. (2000). *The barn owls*. Somersworth, MA: Charlesbridge Publishing.

Kasza, K. (2003). *My lucky day*. New York: Putnam Juvenile.

Keats, E. J. (1998). *A letter to Amy*. New York: Puffin Books.

Keats, E. J. (1998). *Peter's chair*. New York: Puffin Books.

Keats, E. J. (1999). *Apt. 3*. New York: Puffin Books.

Laminack, L. L. (2004). *Saturdays and teacakes*. Atlanta: Peachtree.

Laminack, L. L. (2007). *Snow day!* Atlanta: Peachtree.

Laminack, L. L. (2014). *Three hens and a peacock*. Atlanta: Peachtree.

Lester, H. (2002). *Hooway for Wodney Wat*. Boston: Walter Lorraine Books.

Locker, T. (1997). *Water dance*. Orlando, FL: Harcourt Children's Books.

Lovell, P. (2001). *Stand tall, Molly Lou Melon*. New York: Putnam.

Lyon, G. E. (1990). *Come a tide*. New York: Orchard Paperbacks.

MacLachlan, P. (1994). *All the places to love*. New York: HarperCollins.

MacLachlan, P. (1998). *What you know first*. New York: HarperTrophy.

McLerran, A. (2004). *Roxaboxen*. New York: HarperTrophy.

O'Neill, A. (2002). *The recess queen*. New York: Scholastic.

Rankin, L. (1996). *The handmade alphabet*. New York: Puffin Books.

Raschka, C. (1993). *Yo! Yes?* New York: Scholastic.

Reynolds, P. H. (2004). *Ish*. Cambridge, MA: Candlewick.

Rylant, C. (1998). *Scarecrow*. Orlando, FL: Harcourt Children's Books.

Rylant, C. (2000). *In November*. Orlando, FL: Harcourt Children's Books.

Salley, C. (2002). *Epossumondas*. Orlando, FL: Harcourt Children's Books.

Siebert, D. (2001). *Mississippi*. New York: HarperCollins.

Waring, R. (2001). *Hungry hen*. New York: HarperCollins.

Weatherford, C. B. (2007). *Birmingham, 1963*. Honesdale, PA: Wordsong.

Webb, S. (2004). *Tanka tanka skunk!* London: Orchard Books.

Woodson, J. (2001). *The other side*. New York: Putnam Juvenile.

Woodson, J. (2012). *Each kindness*. New York: Nancy Paulsen Books.

Young, E. (1992). *Seven blind mice*. New York: Philomel.

Index